THE DYING OF ED MEES

A NOVELLA

LINDA A LAVID

plum barn press

REVIEWS FOR THE DYING OF ED MEES

~

I absolutely loved this book! Less about dying and more about living in the moment. Such a fun, captivating read! I laughed. I cried. I was sorry when it was over.

~

Ed Mees is dying; or is he? This is a fast and interesting read that looks at one man's journey toward our shared destination but one which is rarely explored. A serious story, told with humor and humanity.

~

With "The Dying of Ed Mees," Lavid doesn't just break the fourth wall between author and reader, she gleefully pole vaults over it, bringing readers along for a fascinating insight as to how her mind and process work.

~

Loved the characters, the questions posed, the answers hinted at, the journey they took. Funny, touching. The relationships are almost too real.

CHAPTER 1

*D*ear Reader, I'm channeling a character. It's what I do. I'm a writer, who sits and stares, waiting for sparks of inspiration to break into a coherent thought. The key is to allow, never force, because divine guidance, at first, is fragile—a translucent veil, a distant echo—such that the moment one reaches and grabs, it is no longer. But I've learned a trick. I start writing...

In my mind, there is a man. His name is Ed Mees. He's dying. He doesn't want to tell his story, but I'm here nevertheless. To write down what he says, interpret what he means, listen, and hold him if necessary. Although, I'm hoping it won't be necessary. Chin up, I say to myself, to him. I want to document his thinking and how he's feeling. I want to learn something so when my time comes, I'll be ready. Or readier. Or not so afraid.

He's smiling. A guinea pig, he thinks. Sure, why not.

"So what are you dying of?" I ask.

"Does it matter?" he says.

It's a curiosity we have. To know what's killing us. To make sense of the disease, accident, murder, suicide so that

1

they may be avoided, so we may have some false sense of control, so lightning doesn't strike twice. This, however, is not rational.

Imagine a city from a helicopter view where everything is connected but randomly moving: jaywalkers crossing the street, cars driving at different speeds, and lights of all kinds going off in no particular order for reasons you have no way of knowing. And imagine what you don't see. Underground tunnels, people in houses, elevators, office buildings, schools, hospitals, and restaurants. Not to mention all the flora and fauna. And consider even further how each person can affect anything they bump into or are thrown against. It's an impossible feat to know or understand or control a city.

NOW IMAGINE the city is your body with crazy activity unable to be fathomed, where things happen for reasons, but those reasons are not knowable. Still, when we learn of lung cancer, we wonder if there was smoking involved, and if we're not smokers, we breathe a sigh of relief. Whew, we dodged the bullet on that one. But have we? Pollutants, minuscule time bombs are everywhere, gnarly molecules of destructive atoms with odd-numbered electrons eager to attach themselves to our soft, vulnerable bodies via contami-nated air, food, water, and the exchange of bodily fluids that—

"Ahem," Mr. Mees says. "Aren't we supposed to be having a conversation here?"

"Sorry," I say. We are staring at each other. "Have you ever had an MRI? Those things creep me out."

"Why is that?"

"I'm claustrophobic."

"Bummer," he says. "Fear's a bitch."

And we are kindred spirits, two strangers intersecting on an emotional level. This rarely happens unless both of us are in a disastrous situation, shell-shocked, blind to what's coming, and desperate to find common ground for strength, solace, and support. Our scenario? He's dying. Aren't we all?

"What are you afraid of?" I ask. It seems a rhetorical question.

"Lots of things. My ex-wife and spiders mostly."

Hmm...he doesn't mention dying—a stoic.

I say, "Most men don't like spiders. And your ex-wife. At least you're not living with her."

"That's funny," Mr. Mees says with a grin. "I probably see her more now than when we were married. She's interjected herself back into my life. First, she took me for the treatments. Now we go shopping, and she washes my underwear."

"So why are you afraid of her?"

"It's complicated."

And I nod. Relationships have that tendency.

"Cancer," he says, picking up an abandoned thread. "It's spreading, moving along, gathering speed."

Suddenly I'm not sure I want to write this book. Maybe talking about this stuff makes it worse. Or makes me uncomfortable. Or makes me feel guilty, like an ambulance chaser after she signs people up, sues, and gets a nice fat check. Riding on coattails has disadvantages. On the other hand, who am I kidding? I don't make money on books.

"Sounds rough," I say.

He nods. "Some days. But it was worse when I was going for those damn drips. Watching people turn gray and feeling like crap. Then I had to listen to the techs. Blah. Blah. Blah. And see those damn smiley faces everywhere. Add Helen, my wife, wondering where she could get a decent cup of coffee."

I laugh. A stoic and a comedian.

"It's a matter of degrees and time passing," he says. "Some

days, I wake up feeling pretty good, then bam, a few seconds later, I remember I'm dying. But things aren't so bad after I have a cup of coffee on the porch and watch the birds. Until I get a pain, a reminder, and get pissed. It's a flowy thing."

"Yes. I understand. There are times when I think I'm going to die. I start thinking about my breath stopping. And when I think of my breath stopping, I have to remember to breathe, and that's all I can think about. Breathing. And I freak out. My heart pounds. I begin to pant, get lightheaded, and my hands go numb. This goes on for about five minutes until I'm exhausted."

"That's messed up," he says. "Especially since you're not dying."

"I have an overactive imagination."

"You're nuts."

He says it kindly, with a wry smile. And suddenly, I feel an epistemological discussion coming on. Not about death but about perception. Theoretically, what's the difference between one person dying and another who thinks he's dying?

"You're kidding, right?" he says.

I realize Mr. Mees has access to my thoughts. For he is me, and I am him. This could get sticky. There's a reason why mind reading is an ability restricted to the rare psychic. If everyone woo-wooed, we'd all be psychological basket cases defending our impure, incomplete, absurd thoughts. Privacy of mind is our first inalienable right—and primary survival mechanism. Bad enough, we roll our eyes.

"So are you suggesting," Mr. Mees says, "being blind is the same as wearing a blindfold?"

A stoic, comedian, and Zen master. Heavy hitter all around. Not sure I'm capable of continuing.

"You wanna drink?" he says.

And I'm back in. "What da ya got?"

CHAPTER 2

*D*reams. Dear Reader, what are they? What purpose do they serve? Sure, have the scientific community dabble and head to Mars for a look-see, examine the effects of unknown matter-less energies, or weave the virtual world into the real world for some sensory experience. But what about that stuff that happens nightly? Shouldn't somebody be working on this? Anyway, after years of horrific nightmares, I came across a few crumbs of insight. To understand dreams, consider you are everyone and everything in the dream, which leads me to the act of writing.

When writing, I am a quick-change artist embedded in every character. I breathe life into them and—this is the best part—slap them around. Anyway, Ed is not alone in our story. There is another character knocking at the door.

Her name is Roberta Hay. She is 55 years old and divorced. Her 34-year-old daughter, Jenna, also lives in the house with her daughter Rosey, age 12. Their current struggle is how to arrange food in the refrigerator. Roberta eats whatever's on sale. Her daughter only eats food labeled organic. And Rosey is presently enticed by tuna fish, ramen noodles, and chocolate pudding.

Roberta is a self-publishing writer and blogger, re-purposed after thirty years as a newspaper reporter. She must earn a paycheck for the next seven years until the magical age of 62 and social security. The subject of death has been an ever-constant companion to Roberta.

It began oddly after she gave birth to Jenna. It wasn't her own death but the imagined death of her child, Jenna, that became the unrivaled source of anxiety and fear. Things got further convoluted after Rosey was born. Then she had to worry about two of her babies wandering the world, vulnerable to terrorist attacks, killer bees, falling meteors, drunk drivers, food/drug contamination, and a vast litany of anatomical mishaps and biological infestations of viruses, bacteria, deer ticks, to name a few.

Roberta's coping skills have been stellar, given the circumstances. But when one's life has a purpose, no matter what the point is, there is meaning, and meaning makes life worth living. On the other hand, it could be argued that the brunt of Roberta's obsession has fallen on the first and second generations of her offspring, who have had to endure countless warnings about inclement weather, anecdotal oddities rehashed from police scanners, doomsday prophesies from alternative rags, and the worst—horrifying urban legends of stolen kidneys, roasted fetuses, and killers who murder based on a draw from a deck of cards.

Ironically, with so much gloomy doom, Roberta is not particularly fearful of her death. In fact, she's almost ready. All the legal forms are filed with the Surrogate's court: will, power of attorney, and DNR (do not resuscitate). She has designated organ donation on her driver's license; picked out the music for her funeral (Pachelbel); and has decided to be cremated with the ashes cast into her garden, where several pets have found their resting place. She pays a monthly life insurance policy to cover all burial expenses, including a brunch with prime rib and an open bar at The Golden Eagle. She has a gun on contingency if she needs to check out sooner due to pain, dementia, dialysis, or dizziness. And she continues to write and rewrite her obituary. With poetic license, here's where it stands: To those who knew and loved Roberta, her manner of death was unremarkable. Lightening didn't strike. She wasn't bitten by a rabid raccoon or hit by a drunk driver. Her passing occurred in bed, alone, during a Seinfeld rerun. She particularly likes passing. That will never be edited out.

In any event, a month before meeting us, Roberta had been in her office/bedroom writing a freelance article titled: "Prostate Cancer, What Your Doctor Isn't Telling You." The title was attention-getting, albeit a bit distressing. But that's how reporters roll.

The general gist was that diagnosing prostate cancer is more of an art than a science, meaning whether one has or has not prostate cancer is up for interpretation which in turn means that going from an alive state to a dying state is based on a number that may not represent anything. This suggests treatment options could be questionable at best, and overkill at worst, thereby putting patients and their families through the wringer.

But such are the ways of modern medicine. In the old days, when someone got sick, he took herbs. Sometimes he'd feel better, sometimes not. Then one day...poof. Today, when someone feels sick, he sees a doctor, goes for tests, and treatments, feels sicker and weaker, takes herbs, to then...poof.

This got Roberta thinking about how one navigates the long second act of dying with its slow descent into the world of sterile places, interminable waits, people with clipboards, needles, instruments, machines, and, if one was lucky, the occasional joke. Then the brainstorm. How about a series of articles, perhaps even a blog, that documents one person's journey, bringing to the fore the renowned stages of death described by Elizabeth Kübler-Ross? Maudlin, yes. But with universal adverse appeal. Or at least appeal to her. And in the days that followed, Roberta worked on a plan. It was not smooth sailing.

The first problem was finding the right person. She already had a list: a shout-out to her reporter friends; inquiries into hospital support groups; a general announcement on Craigslist; discrete visits to cancer social media groups. But then she thought of another snag. She'd have to offer something in return. Money wasn't an option for two reasons. First, she didn't have any. Secondly, the promise of a future, vague enumeration from a book, movie, or foreign rights deal, seemed ridiculous given the circumstances.

Then, just this morning, she had an epiphany. She could find someone who needed help, then provide that help. A partnership. A barter system where she would render free rides to medical appointments with a hand to hold, and, in return, they would be interviewed, taped, photographed, filmed. Who'd pass that up?

CHAPTER 3

*D*ear Reader, in manipulating characters, a writer finds herself watchful, curious, and, at times, mischievous. She pulls strings like a puppeteer. It's a fun pastime of pretending. But at some point, critical mass is reached, and a character takes on a life, purpose, and personality that is, to some extent, separate from the string puller.

I say 'to some extent' because all characters remain extensions, tributaries of the writer in one way or another. As writers sit on their behinds, characters do the heavy lifting, exploring the good, evil, brave, cowardly, loving, hateful, etc., in a contrived environment of simulated reality.

And I wonder why we, the writer and reader, are so drawn to such pretending (pretension). Shouldn't we be dealing with our immediate issues? Food, clothing, shelter, and Maslow's Hierarchy of Needs as it ascends to self-actualization? But then I understand. Somehow, in some ways, fake stories are the ironic vehicles to truth and understanding.

Now to Mr. Mees, who is conveniently dying.

When I first met him, we talked, or mostly I talked. He is a quiet man who listens remarkably well. He didn't try to solve any of my problems. He just nodded on occasion and sipped his drink. Perhaps he wasn't listening. Does it matter? There's something about getting crap out of head space. Maybe, 'Bless me, Father, for I have sinned' does, after all, have prophylactic benefits. In any event, I will not be scrapping Mr. Mees. He's a hero, true and steady—the strong silent type.

Anyway, hovering in his world like a Chagall painting, I now find Mr. Mees in the kitchen. He has a stack of mail, mostly flyers and advertising, to go through. He'd like to chuck the lot, but there may be some medical stuff he needs to read and get confused by.

"So you're back," he says.

I'm very silent, suspended from the ceiling. Who's he talking to?

He looks up. "You, the Manhattan lady."

At first, I'm confused. Then I understand. He was referring to the drink he had offered me. I say hello.

"Couldn't stay away?"

"No. You're under my skin."

"Me? Why do you think?"

"I'm curious."

"Curiosity is a good thing. If there weren't any, we'd still live in caves figuring out how to boil water."

"I think you have hero potential."

He laughs. "Potential? Sounds sketchy. We're all heroes at one time or another."

Now I remember why I've returned. He makes me feel good. And I float down to where he sits.

Meeting a person for the first time is exciting, new, and full of discovery. But there's an oddness here. We are not looking to find someone too different from ourselves. Instead, we search for similarity, common ground, mutual understanding, and a hanging-out partner. Then it happens.

It could take minutes, months, or years. Suddenly, a new friend is not a friend but someone unlikable and full of shortcomings. However, for the time being, Mr. Mees and I are in the getting-to-know-you phase, where judgment is temporarily suspended, and charm abounds.

So who is Mr. Mees? What's he about?

Foregoing the urge to discuss his birth sign and get mired in rising and retrograde planets, I search for clues in his environment, specifically, his person and belongings, where a treasure trove of information is found.

At the back door, one set of paired shoes sits neatly on a mat. Above, an equally singular jacket and umbrella hang from two hooks. There are no dishes to be done. He is fully dressed, wearing a tucked-in plaid shirt and khakis. A lone kitchen window with cafe curtains is the only light source on this cloudy day. Without bothering to turn on the overhead, Mr. Mees is a shadow in the kitchen.

"It hums," Mr. Mees says.

"Excuse me?"

"The light. It has an annoying hum. Reminds me of the hospital."

"I see," I say.

He relaxes into the chair. "I should warn you. There's not much going on around here."

Dear Reader, for the first time, Mr. Mees is flat-out wrong. There's a ton going on. Not only are we, you and I, in discovery, but we sit at a precipice, on edge, in anticipation. It's an exciting place to be. Not knowing what will happen but believing something will. And not just anything but something remarkable. How do I know this? I feel it. I got a nose for it. Otherwise, I wouldn't have started. There's a string being pulled here. A tiny thread of seemingly little consequence. It's attached to something hidden, distant, buried, but inevitable as sure as gravity.

"I have confidence in you," I say.

"Confidence?"

"That you'll deliver."

He laughs. "Sure, that isn't your job?"

"Tell you what," I say. "This is your game. You're in charge. Would you like that?"

Mr. Mees stares off for a moment. He's thinking. He's being seduced. Control of one's destiny is not easily passed up.

"You mean I will decide what happens to me?" He seems incredulous.

"Yes," I say and let go of the reins. It's exhilarating to ride a horse without reins.

CHAPTER 4

*H*ere we are in a McDonald's parking lot where I am orchestrating a coincidental meeting between my characters. This makes me wonder if some entity is doing the same to me on another level in another dimension. Could this be possible? Could all of us be here due to the imaginings of some quirky writer driven by alcohol and an overprotective mother? It's not so farfetched and could explain the notion of earthly coincidences, like that weird unexplainable moment of seeing the hermit who lives next door in an airport three thousand miles away.

However, to consider my life as someone's thought is, well, obscene. Emphatically, I am not a furry patch in a Petri dish floating in sugar and excrement who only exists for someone's amusement to work out her issues or transcribe my dismal life choices into an overly dramatized Lifetime movie. Excuse me, but there's a mind within this tired, old body. A person with thoughts, feelings, and, dare I say, free will.

Still, the parallels between being a writer and a character are becoming remarkably similar in my mind. My characters also have free will, albeit given certain constructs, parameters. They are free to act within limits, that is to say, my limits.

Now that I realize I could exist only in thought, as a character in some other mind, I'll have to check Google to see if this is remotely possible. Those physicists are always coming up with strange theories. Death is terrible but having my existence be some random thought is worse. Whoa. I need to calm down, reel myself in, think logically, and dive back into my orchestrated narrative.

Mr. Mees loves McDonald's. He loves the uncomplicated menu, the efficiency of service, the anchored molded plastic chairs, the clean bathrooms, and, most of all, the cheap cup of coffee that's always hot and strong. It's the one place besides his home and yard where he can go, order, sit, and be.

Ms. Hay knows all the McDonald's within a twenty-mile radius of her home if she needs to use a restroom. She has a fussy stomach prone to Hershey squirts, those indelicate attacks of intestinal eruptions that demand immediate attention and release.

On this particular day, we find Mr. Mees and Ms. Hay backing out from their respective parking spots. A large van sits between them, blocking a clear view. Mr. Mees swerves to the left. Ms. Hay swerves to the right. Within seconds, the two cars collide with a crunch and jolt.

Fender-benders are curious events. Just enough drama to evaluate one's mettle and see what drivers are made of. Naturally, our two friends react differently. Cool, calm, and dying, Ed pulls back into his spot. Roberta, on the other hand, refuses to budge. First, she does a body scan, checking for pain, blood, and immovable parts. Then she reaches for her phone. Pictures need to be taken, and 911 called.

Five minutes later, they are inside, waiting for the police

to arrive. Ed has purchased two cups of coffee. Chit-chat turns to occupations.

Roberta responds to Ed. "I'm a writer."

"Are you making a living at that?"

"Sort of. And yourself?"

"Retired from the railroad."

Roberta nods. "Good for you. They have nice pensions."

"Can't complain. Do you work for the papers?"

"Not anymore. I'm a freelancer. Do human interest stories, then sell them to the highest bidder."

"I see. Nice to be your own boss."

"Would be nicer if I made more money."

"And what would you do with more money?"

"Excuse me?"

"If you made more money, how would you spend it?"

"I'd pay bills."

"I see," says Ed. "Being in debt is stressful."

"Well, I'm not in debt. I just have bills to pay."

"So you're paying your bills. I mean, you can afford your bills. That's a good thing. That should make you happy."

"Happy?"

Mr. Mees doesn't respond. The conversation is reminiscent of similar interactions with his ex-wife. He takes a sip of coffee and looks out the window for a patrol car.

Roberta also doesn't particularly care for the man. Mostly because she's jealous that she's got seven more years to work, and this guy is living off the fat of the land with an exorbitant pension.

And she makes other assumptions.

First, he lives alone. There is no wedding band on his finger or wife in the car. Second, he's cheap. Hell, if you want breakfast, there's the Big Slam at Denny's. Third, he's a slob. What does it take to get an electric razor and do a quick pass?

More minutes fill the void.

Ed Mees jumps back in. "What exactly is a human interest story?"

"They're stories about people who have remarkable things happen. Something unusual or hopeful or heroic. Anything that tugs at your heart."

"I see," Ed says. "So, how do you find these stories?"

"Usually from other articles. Sometimes people I know from the business give me tips."

"And what are you working on now?"

"I'm researching the dying process."

Mr. Mees puts down the coffee cup. His heart is starting to race. He feels like something, some entity, is messing with him. Of all the people in town, he had to run into a death freak.

I keep still.

Roberta continues. "I know it sounds like a downer, but I think people could benefit by addressing this issue sooner than later."

This issue sticks in Ed's craw. "What do you know about dying?"

"I think about it every day."

"And why is that?"

"My family says I'm a worrywart."

"But why do you think about it so much?"

Roberta shrugs. "I don't know."

Insight into our behaviors is often unknowable. We go through experiences that change how we think, act, respond. While our adaptability is a strength, it is also a weakness. We manage to absorb shocks and move along, but injury, harm, distress, and fear sift into our bodies, brains, hearts and burrow beneath the surface. But there are always buoys marking the spot. A teenager who sucks her thumb. A businessman who grinds his teeth. And yes, intestinal distress.

Roberta has long forgotten the origin of her obsession. In fact, it's become such a part of her that without it, she wouldn't know who she'd be. And therein lies a dilemma. Maladjusted behaviors create odd but persistent comfort levels. Poor Roberta. Poor humanity.

"Anyway, I got some ideas. I want to do a series of articles, a running series, a documentary on someone dying. What their life's like. How it's changing them. You know, get in their head."

"How is this a human interest story?"

"Good question." Roberta's face lights up. "People get sick, suffer, die, and no one knows what the hell to do, how to act. Death has become too removed from everyday life. People are dying, and no one says a word to them. Is that fair? And how are they supposed to prepare? A person should know more than less. And sooner than later."

"Would you want to know?"

"Definitely."

Ed leans over to her. "Can I tell you a secret?"

Roberta meets him halfway.

Ed whispers, "You are dying. We all are."

Roberta smiles. "Touché. But seriously. Take yourself, for instance. Would you want to know?"

"Actually, I do know."

"Huh? Know what?"

"That I'm dying."

"You mean you're really dying?"

"Apparently."

"Who told you?"

"My doctor. He says about six months."

Roberta sits back in the chair. Ed can't be sure what's percolating. Meanwhile, a police car has pulled into the lot. Luckily, time's run out on their tête à tête.

CHAPTER 5

*D*ear Reader, I used to think life would be far more manageable if we could program our dreams. Starving during the day? Go to sleep and enjoy an eight-course meal. Wanna murder someone? Do it at night and never serve time. And, as far as sex. That would be wide open. Johnny Depp, Marilyn Monroe, twins, sheiks, at any time, in any position. But then I realized the problem. If we could manipulate our dreams, we'd never want to wake up.

Which leads me to death and the fear of dying. If we didn't fear death, many of us would throw ourselves off cliffs. Few would make it to old age, let alone high school graduation. So here we are, dealing with death and its attendant fear. Yes, perhaps it's the fear of death that keeps us alive. Mind-bending. But truths often are.

Two days after Ed and Roberta met, Ed's at home sitting on the front porch. It's around ten in the morning when he hears his name being called. "Ed, how are you doing?"

Down a couple of houses, a woman is waving. It looks like she just got out of a car because she's in the middle of the road. Even though she doesn't look familiar, Ed waves. As she closes in, shit is heard inside his head.

"Hey, there, stranger. Remember me? We met at McDonald's. I was in the neighborhood and figured I'd stop by and see how you're doing."

Ed's not sure how to respond. Or what she may be referring to.

She's climbing up the porch steps. "Mind if I sit? Won't stay long."

"I guess," Ed says.

She eases into the other Adirondack chair. "I just wanted to thank you for our little talk. It helped me formulate my plan. I will still do the story, but I will supersize it."

"Well, I'm sure you'll do a grand job." Mr. Mees is looking at a bright red cardinal. Funny how they never come to the feeder. Just stand by and go for any seeds that fall.

"OK. Our first plan of attack will be on social media. This way, everything can be fed to multiple outlets. And since I have a ton of articles, I'll dovetail them in. For instance, if we want to talk about medical testing, I can toss in my prostate stuff. Or we mention herbs, and I can segue to my alternative medicine articles..."

Did Ed hear the word "we" on two occasions? "Excuse me, Ms. Hay—"

"Please call me Roberta."

Ed manages a nod. "Roberta, when you say 'we,' what exactly do you mean?"

"You and me, of course."

"So I'm your human interest story?"

"No. Co-author. Fifty, fifty all the way."

Ed smirks. "Roberta, I'm not interested."

"But that's why I'm here, Ed. I can call you Ed, right?" Oblivious to any response, she continues, "I'm here to convince you."

Her honesty makes Ed smile. "And how are you going to do that?"

"I'm a reporter and a damn good one. I never take no for an answer. In fact, I like the pushing and shoving."

"Well. I hate to disappoint you, but that won't be necessary. The answer is no."

"I can help you."

"Help me? With what?"

"Anything you like. I'll be here for you. We'll deal with this together."

Loopy, Ed thinks. What's this lady's angle?

"Listen. I did a little research. You're alone, except for your ex-wife. Your son lives in Harrietstown and never visits. You had some friends at the Moose, but you stopped going about a month ago. No church affiliations. And the only neighbor who stops by is Tony Parisi asking for beer money."

"How do you know about Tony?"

"Facebook."

"Roberta, you sound more like the FBI than a reporter. That makes me very uncomfortable. The answer is no. Sorry."

There's a smile on Roberta's face. A frozen smile. She then regains composure. "I understand. If you ever change your mind, here's my card." And she burrows through her purse.

"By the way, how did you find me?" he asks.

"Police report. Did you call your insurance company?"

"No."

"You really should call them." She hands him her card.

"Why?"

"To file a claim and fix the damage."

"Can't be bothered."

Roberta nods. "I understand," and she holds out her hand. Her grasp is warm and firm. "Pleasure talking with you."

Minutes later, Roberta is down the street, unlocking the car door, and Ed is putting sunflower seeds in the feeder.

From a distance, they are two lone people seemingly unaffected, unchanged. But this isn't true. Their lives have intersected, and they can't now, or in the future, be complete strangers. Intimacies of body language and the exchange of information have left their mark. Assumptions and impressions have tainted the waters. In the murkiness, judgment follows.

Mr. Mees is relieved she's gone.

Ms. Hay knows she'll be back.

CHAPTER 6

*D*ear Reader, to imagine. What greater gift is there? Where all is possible. Yet imagination is sorely undervalued, even discouraged, outlawed. According to some, there is danger in imagination. Freedom of thought is chaos, rule-breaking, belief-shattering, and a huge waste of time when you could be watching reruns.

Imagine too much, too often, and you will sink into perverse quicksands from which there is no salvation. Imagine at your own risk, at your own sanity, for you are playing with fire. Fire, I might add, radiates heat and light.

In any event, I have been relying on your imagination to fathom what my characters look like. Shall we compare?

In my mind, Mr. Mees is in his late sixties, still robust with thinning hair but enough to part and comb. He is not going to seed, as Ms. Hay had implied when she commented on his stubble. On that particular day, he had been awake since four in the morning, and by the time he left the house to get coffee, his entire morning routine was messed up. Consider Mr. Mees looking like the present-day Robert De

Niro, only not so smoldering, more of a character actor than a star.

Roberta Hay is a bundle of scattered energy who takes her granddaughter's advice on the cut and color of her hair, the length and style of clothes, and what shade to use on her nails, lips, and eyes. This translates into a woman unafraid of purple, magenta, and large print patterns. This morning, with subtle pink highlights in her hair, she is wearing a full-skirted floral dress accessorized with flip-flops, blue toenails, and shimmery bronze lip gloss. She's around a size twelve in women's. She and Rosey often go to boutiques where nothing quite fits but is close enough for her.

So here they are. A man. A woman. Both single and of a certain age. I suspect you may be thinking a romance is brewing. However, since romance isn't my strength, it's not my intention. On the other hand, I could use my imagination. Or better yet, I'll let the characters do their thing while I sit back and transcribe.

Since our last encounter, Mr. Mees has not been feeling well. He's exhausted, bone tired, and sleeping a lot.

He's thinking of going to the Moose at around five to get out and have a real meal, a fish fry. If he can't eat the whole thing, he'll bring some home. In the middle of formulating a plan, the doorbell rings. From the vestibule, Ed sees an unfamiliar young girl. It must be Girl Scout Cookie time. When he opens the door, Roberta is standing next to the girl.

"Hey, Ed. This is my granddaughter, Rosey. "Say 'hello,' Rosey."

The girl smiles tightly and waves. Ed assumes she has braces.

Ed doesn't move. Not in or out. He stands firm. On guard. "What can I do for you, Roberta?"

"We were shopping, and I saw the most remarkable thing.

I thought of you and decided to buy it." She then hands him a plastic bag. "You'll get a kick out of it."

"I don't—"

"No strings attached."

Rosey, the granddaughter, is now grinning. Her mouth is full of metal.

Inside the bag is a figure of a man covered in birdseed. A red string is wrapped around the figure's feet. The fat lettering says Bungee Bird Feeder.

Mr. Mees smiles.

"Rosey will help you hang it."

Out in the yard, there's a general pow-wow. Rosey thinks the man should be thrown over the branch, then slip-knotted. Roberta suggests grabbing a lower limb, pulling it down, then tying the red string. While the two are rambling, Ed gets the ladder from the garage. Soon the bungee feeder is hanging. It looks like an upside-down cross. Ed suspects it may be blasphemous to some. Hopefully, Helen won't notice.

"We'll be off," Roberta says.

Ed is lost for words. He doesn't want to encourage her by being too friendly or appreciative. He also has trouble being rude. He says, "Sure thing. Bye now."

Back in the car, Rosey says, "Mr. Mees doesn't look like he's dying."

"Sometimes it's hard to tell."

"I think he liked what we gave him."

"Really? What makes you say so?"

"He was careful putting it up. Away from the squirrels so they couldn't jump to it or climb down on it. Are we going to keep giving him stuff?"

"I think so. Now that you met him, what do you think he'd like?"

Rosey bit the edge of her lip. "Maybe some socks with birds."

"Great idea!"

~

THREE HOURS LATER, Mr. Mees has returned home from the Moose club. Besides dinner, he's had a few beers. It's dark, and the porch light casts long shadows onto the front yard. As he approaches the steps, he notices, from the corner of his eye, a movement across the lawn. Curious, he steps over. Then he sees. Above the spot from the moving pattern on the lawn, the bungee feeder, looking tortured, is wavering in the breeze.

Seeing a replicated human hanging by his feet, alone, swaying in darkness is disconcerting and sure to cause one of his troubling nightmares, a side effect of medication no matter how many berries the doctor has recommended him to eat before bedtime. He needs to rip the nasty thing down or at least cut off the string and prop the figure on a branch for any bird, chipmunk, or squirrel to ravage.

He reaches for the upside-down man, but it's too high and only grazes his fingertips. With each swat, the bungee figurine moves faster across the axis like a pendulum, making it more difficult to grab.

Not one to give up, Mr. Mees waits. As the bird feeder slows and begins to settle at its lowest point, he jumps...and misses. On his descent, his knees crumble, and he lands abruptly on his rear. Looking up, he sees and concludes the swaying, mocking feeder is blatantly unconcerned. Son of a bitch. He's been beaten by a ridiculous inanimate object. Dejected, he doesn't have the energy to get up.

Mr. Mees can't remember the last time he's sat on the ground. His towering home looks overbearing, uninviting, and scarily unfamiliar. The only light on the porch is no longer a beacon, but a dimming wick of a worn-down candle, like so much of his life and what it has become, dark with fewer markers to hold him steady and in charge. He thinks of standing, but why? And he eases down to lie flat on his back.

The ground is cool and damp. The tree branches are tentacles reaching across the starless, moonless sky. He is the last man on earth. He searches for the upside-down hanging man. It's now still and unmoving.

His body is a heavy mass, weighted down, immobilized, and melded into the ground from the gravitational pull. He lifts his arm and feels the drag. Its weight is cumbersome. He allows the arm to fall. Yes. Perhaps, he's had too much to drink. Perhaps.

He shuts his eyes and listens, the most passive activity he can manage now. The night is soundless, except for a whooshing. It's coming from inside his head. He tries to shake it out. It gets louder.

Whoosh. Whoosh. It's pumping blood, pressurized, he imagines, stretching apart a sinewy capillary or two, where in certain worn sections, the thin sidewalls are bulging, ready to blow.

And a rising panic gathers speed. It's the recurrent reality. He's fucking dying. His heart races at the thought of nothingness, a paralyzed state of pitch-black oblivion where he is trapped, gagged, and bound for eternity. Calm down. That's ridiculous. Is he even going to know when he's dead? Best be more concerned about that moment of death, the final breath. Christ. He gasps.

The heaviness in his chest radiates out. First into his shoulders, then beyond into his arms. He tries to inhale, but instead of breathing in, the air is squeezed out. Damn. This is it on the front lawn of all places. He lies in frozen fear as the aching pressure fills his body. How much pain will he have to endure? Whoosh. Whoosh. Whoosh.

He must prepare himself, but his body is coming apart too quickly. And his mind? It's tumbling with flashes of incidents in his life. Images that speed by in less than a blink. In confusion, he tries to grab any comforting picture. But the birth of his son is gone before he has a chance. The ache in his chest is now burning. He thinks of his mother. And calls out her name. Suddenly, a curtain falls.

Dear Reader, while Mr. Mees is in a remarkable state, he is not dead. Not yet. He's having a cardiac incident, deeply affected by converging forces, subterranean and otherwise, of which he does not know and is ignorant.

Yes. The heart, the receptacle of human emotion, is sorely misunderstood in these modern times, where it is casually treated as a pumping muscle of parts replaced, lines excavated, and cells electrified, so everything else can run smoothly. And it agrees to manipulation because, from the beginning, from its first beat, it only wants the best for us.

Mr. Mees opens his eyes. The building pressure inside is a soft mass of wavering water. There is no chest pain, no noise inside his head. Still, there is an oddity. It's uncontrollable. Ed is weeping. Not because he's dying or in pain or alone. He's crying because while he has made mistakes, had regrets, passed along blame, and taken on guilt, there has always been, in some way, kindness to see him through.

Through a curtain of tears, the bungee bird feeder hangs solidly. Ed is thankful from the bottom of his heart.

CHAPTER 7

*D*ear Reader, it's best to leave out the boring parts in fiction. Mundane activities like brushing teeth, making dinner, or taking a shower are best done by characters in the privacy of the author's mind. As Hemingway said, "Never confuse movement with action." Still, as a counterpoint, juxtaposing boring parts with change carries a punch in fiction, as in life.

It's dinner time at Roberta's house. Jenna is making a salad, and Roberta is checking for a chicken breast recipe online. Hers always tastes like shoe leather. She's scrolling down to find something new. Her eyes stop at Chicken Paprikash with Greek Yogurt. This could be it.

"Mother," Jenna says. "We have to talk."

Roberta's reading the ingredients: onions, carrots, chicken stock. She'll use bullion. And for the scallions. How about dried chives?

"Are you listening?"

"Yes," Roberta says with distraction.

"I don't want Rosey going with you to visit strange men."

Roberta's attention can't be diverted. "Jenna, can I use a

cup of your Greek yogurt? This recipe looks great. Want to see the picture?"

"Mom, are you listening?"

Roberta wonders. Was that cayenne pepper or paprika buried in the spice cabinet?

"Mother!"

Roberta looks up.

"Did you hear what I said?"

Roberta shakes her head. "Sorry."

"I don't want you taking Rosey to see strange men."

"What strange men?"

"That guy."

"Mr. Mees? But he's harmless. Besides Rosey would never be alone with him. I'm there."

"That's not the point."

Roberta looks at her daughter. "Well, what is the point?"

"He's...you know..."

"What?"

"Dying. What if you go to his house, and he's stiff as a board?"

"That's ridiculous. He wouldn't be able to come to the door."

Jenna lets out an exasperated sigh. "Mother, I'm so sick of this death stuff. I've learned to live with it, but now it's being passed onto Rosey. That's all she talks about. It's too much."

"Rosey is very well-rounded and insightful and caring. You should be proud of her."

"Yes. She is very caring. But what happens if she gets attached, as she did with her father?"

"Her father isn't dead."

"Mother, it's about loss. How much do you think she'll be able to handle? Besides, she needs to be a regular kid. Not some ghoul with a death obsession. Before long, she'll only wear black, and all her friends will be suicidal."

"She hates black."

Jenna stares dryly at Roberta.

Roberta knows the look and feels a familiar tension rising into her neck. A confrontation is brewing. Will she be able to deter, deflect, or decelerate a head-on collision? She averts her eyes to the recipe. Maybe returning to the mundane will stop all forward motion.

Yes, Dear Reader, perhaps there is familiar ground here where you recognize the mother and daughter pas de deux with its endless loop of advance/retreat in oxymoronic maneuverings of passive resistance, supportive criticism, and tough love, to name a few. In many ways, it can't be avoided.

Mothers and daughters are soldiers-at-arms in a symbiotic leg race, tied together, crippled, while each tries to navigate a lifetime of obstacles, where one leads, and the other follows but neither at the same time and rarely before feelings are hurt, or gloves come off; and where the only one left standing is the one who refuses to move in any direction. Still, they need each other because, without a third party to intervene, to referee, to pull each one aside before the nails come out, it's them against the world.

"Fine," Jenna says. "Pretend you're not listening, but I'm Rosey's mother, and we can be out of here anytime."

Roberta's breath is getting shallow. She glares at her daughter. The words come out remarkably calm. "Don't threaten me, Jenna. If you want to leave, go. As for Rosey, you might consider asking her where she'd rather be."

"Excuse me? I'm her mother."

"You never have time for her."

"What?"

"You heard me."

"Well, excuse me if I have to work."

"I'm not talking about work."

"What? When I go out on Saturday nights?"

Roberta takes a deep breath. "Saturday nights?"

"I'm trying to have a life. Sue me."

There comes a time when a cliff is just a step away. There comes a time when a decision has to be made. Forward or back? Roberta doesn't have the energy on this particular evening.

"Jenna, can we stop this?" Roberta then chooses her words carefully. "I promise to have Rosey stay with you whenever I see Mr. Mees."

Jenna lets out a sigh. "Thank you."

Roberta smiles almost too sweetly. "Now, about that yogurt."

ACROSS TOWN, another family drama careens downhill.

"You want to go fishing out of town?" Ed's ex-wife, Helen, says. "That's crazy. You're in no condition to travel."

"I feel fine."

"But I can't get away. I need to give notice at work and check with—"

"I'm going by myself."

"Excuse me? You can't go by yourself."

"I'm a grown man."

"You need medical approval. Have you spoken with the doctor?"

"Medical approval? For what?"

"To drive."

"I drive every day. The doctor knows that."

"Where are you going? Have you made reservations? And what about your medications?"

Ed braces himself. Haughty rhetorical questions are Helen's way of melding concern with control. Questions that are asked to illuminate how confused he is as if she's talking to a child, as if she's obliquely shedding light on the obvious. But he knows the maneuvers and wades in cautiously.

"I'm heading up north."

"North? Where exactly?"

"Adirondacks."

"You can drive for days and not see anyone. Do you think that's wise?"

"I'll have my phone."

"But will you have reception? What if you need help?"

"I'll start a forest fire."

Helen's face shrinks into a pinched, sour look as if she's taken a bite out of a lemon. He imagines all the muscles beneath her skin have contracted into frozen gnarly knots. It's all too familiar. When was the last time she laughed? Not at his jokes, which had been years, but at any recent time?

"Is that supposed to be funny?" she says.

"Only if you think so."

Helen leans against the kitchen sink and folds her arms. "What the hell is going on?"

How Ed married (and divorced) a woman smarter than he has always confounded him. Or maybe not smarter, just more wolf-like than he, with a hypersensitive nose for bull-shit. He must not cave in. "Nothing's going on."

"Really? When was the last time you went fishing?"

"That's the point. I miss fishing."

"I don't believe it."

Ed knows he's navigating that sliver of space between truth and falsehood, a nebulous area where omission, deflection, and purposeful vagueness secures just enough peace to keep a conversation, and relationship, from tanking. "Helen, I'm a big boy. I got everything covered."

"Covered? Covered up, I'd say. After all, I've done for you...."

Ed stops listening. The conversation is twisting into an

attention-seeking guilt ploy where he is expected to defend his position or apologize for any misunderstanding. He's been here before and has learned from his mistakes.

It's what caused their divorce after twenty-five years, when in an inebriated state, he blurted out, after hours of badgering, that at times he wanted to kill her, not that he had a plan, not that he would, but yes, he had considered it as an option to her relentless inquisitions and accusations.

Dear Reader, it didn't end there. Once verbalized, his rant took on perceived truth that led to papers being served. In turn, he packed one lone bag and headed softly into the spanking new night where he no longer had to deal with their manufactured nonsense, either his or hers.

Helen's words are streaming. "....have I ever heard a thank you? No. Ever a concern about how this is affecting my life? No. I don't...."

He should be paying attention, but he's thinking of his next move. Deflection. Yes. Of course.

"Helen. I do appreciate everything you've done. Thank you. I just need to get out of here. Please."

Her look seems to soften. She nods. "OK. But...well, are you—"

For some odd reason, Helen has stopped mid-sentence. He is curious. "Am I what?"

Her words rush out. "Going to hurt yourself?"

Ed stifles a laugh. "I'm not that bad at fishing."

"Always a joke with you. Fine. Go on your trip."

"Listen, nothing's going to happen. It's only for a few days. When I get back, we'll go out for dinner. Any place you like."

She looks suspicious. "Any place?"

"Yes."

"Promise?"

Ed nods.

Helen suddenly looks happier, younger. Before she leaves, he hugs her, suspecting that, after this trip, it may be the last hug she'll ever allow.

Ten minutes later, he's in the basement collecting the gear —three fishing rods, two tackle boxes, a pair of hip boots, a couple of hats, one vest—and stacks it all on top of the work table. He then unlocks a cabinet for the bait he'll need to catch the biggest fish ever: a Winchester 94, 9mm Glock, and his treasured double barrel Bernadelli Gamecock.

Dear Reader, Ed is not going fishing. Instead, he's going to visit Drew, his son. He's going to try to make amends.

CHAPTER 8

*R*eductionist thinking cuts away tangential, creative exploration into a metaphoric six-lane arterial highway that converges into three, then two lanes where vistas shrink and further still where the road, amid encroaching overgrowth and diminishing traffic, becomes one lane that turns from concrete to asphalt to blacktop to gravel to dirt, to then, as it burrows into oblivion, disappear altogether in the middle of nowhere.

But reductionism isn't just about thought. It can be a way of life experienced firsthand by remaining tethered to the past, stuck in routine of mind and body, unable to change habits or trajectories. And where caught in a tedious maze, life becomes hollow, brittle, and stale. Unless...

Dear Reader, what if any life can be changed by simply making a choice? And what if the menu of options (like fraying threads) exists at all times, simultaneously, ready to be pulled and unraveled for lives to loosen up and expand? What if, at this very moment, you become aware of more than one possibility: an odd thought, a new idea, a different direction? Anyway, it happened to Mr. Mees.

The Friday night after Ed didn't die, he reassembled himself, stood, and wobbled into the house. When he walked through the front door, he stopped. The path forked— upstairs or down? He grabbed the railing and held tight, unsure which way to go, what to do. His thoughts were racing, tumbling.

Ed put his hand on his chest to see if there was any tenderness, any lingering pain. Yes, there was some pressure, more of an ache, a tinge. He could head to the ER and have the dubious pleasure of spending hours with unfamiliar people, some suffering, others bustling around tritely with clipboards and squishy shoes in deceptively antiseptic surroundings. Or he could call Helen, wake her up, and be prepared to answer a litany of probing questions, which, when answered, would be an admission to having a drink or two. Or he could sit tight and take his chances. He had laughed at this as if the Grim Reaper gave chances. Better to hit the bourbon and wait for the takedown with fists in the air. Ed then headed to the buffet, filled a tumbler of whiskey, and sat at the dining room table.

Before long, the ragged edges of the situation turned inward.

Damn. How had he come to this—a pitiful guy with an expanding medical file who quietly, stoically, absorbed such crap: measurements (pressure readings, chemistry panels, blood counts); needles (poking in, drawing out); pills (an assemblage of colorful toxins); and those damn tests, treatments ("You're doing great Mr. Mees.") All for what? Buying the farm on the front lawn? Hell, enough of that shit.

And a curious thought arose from nowhere. The kind of idea that seems spontaneous but, in truth, is the result of a streaming subconscious that connects and links subterranean mishmash into cognition, a loose thread, which led

Mr. Mees, amid his precarious death watch, to wonder: Where was that picture?

Minutes later, Ed fished through a box of photographs taken long ago with a Polaroid. Not seen in years, the snapshots had washed out, most likely encroached upon by subtle chemical changes in the developer, ink, and paper that were further compromised by atmospheric events (humidity, heat, pollution), and microscopic arthropods that bustled and shed and reproduced endlessly across the tacky surface.

Pictures that he then held to the light as forms coalesced. A Thanksgiving dinner with his arm around Helen, both smiling, a happy couple. But he remembered. He had gotten home late that evening, having worked a double shift with a stopover at a bar for shots of Tequila. He looked happy, but he was smashed. Had Helen noticed? What truth is there in photographs? Not much, he decided. They are façades, space holders of time.

And then he found it—a grainy shot of father and son pheasant hunting. Ed, squinting into the sun with the shotgun held high, locked against his shoulder, posed for the picture, posed for posterity. What a joke. Another falsehood.

Ed narrowed his gaze on Drew. His lean, sullen son was hunched over, looking askance into the camera with a borrowed, single-shot Mossberg that hung loosely from the bend of his elbow and pointed to the ground.

Ed recalled the scene's drama as he preened for the camera, and his son just wanted to leave. More pressure filled Ed's chest. Not a pain, a heaviness. Damn, what a jerk he had been. Ed put down the photograph. Tears welled up, then coursed down his cheeks. After minutes of sobbing, the pain in his heart remarkably dissipated. It was then, at one in the morning, in an inebriated, half-dying state, Ed had decided to visit his son in Harrietstown.

As an aside, Dear Reader, contrary to what Mr. Mees

believes, there is truth in photographs. But the trueness comes from the one who observes the picture, not the subject at all. It is about the looker, the seer, the searcher, and what he projects or needs to see.

~

SERENDIPITY HAPPENS. It's a sign for some, a simple coincidence for others, and a mathematical conundrum for those obsessed with probability. It also can be considered rotten luck.

When Roberta, with Rosey in tow, shows up at Ed's on Sunday morning, Mr. Mees is loading his car with fishing gear. Roberta glances at her dashboard clock. It's barely 9 AM. She has showered, gotten Rosey up, stopped for coffee and doughnuts, wrapped the socks, and gone over her attack plan. Well, not an attack but a seductive argument to convince Mr. Mees how working with her would be a win-win proposition.

Rosey turns to her grandmother. "Looks like Mr. Mees is heading out. Are we still going to give him his present?"

"Of course." Roberta backs up a wee bit and then swerves into Mr. Mees's driveway, parking directly behind his car, conveniently blocking any exit for a quick getaway.

Mr. Mees turns.

Roberta waves out the driver's side window. "Hello there. How are you doing today?"

Ed walks toward the car. "Fine. And yourself?"

"Great!" Roberta says.

Ed stoops down and peers at where Rosey is sitting. "And you, young lady?"

Rosey sticks up her thumb and gives him a broad smile.

"Going somewhere?" Roberta asks.

"Yep. Fishing. All ready to go. Sorry. I don't have time to talk. I got a long drive ahead."

"Where to?"

"Adirondacks."

"Wonderful! I picked up some doughnuts and coffee. You can put them in your car. Still hot and fresh. Nothing like having a special treat when you hit the road."

"Thanks, but—"

"No buts about it. Rosey, can you grab the box and one coffee?"

Mr. Mees shakes his head. "No. It's not necessary. I just had breakfast."

Roberta jostles the door open and slips from the car. Her mind is reeling. She must make sure her approach is engaging, non-threatening, and spontaneous. She looks to the sky. "Certainly is a fine day for a ride."

"Yes."

"Will Mrs. Mees be joining you?" she asks innocently. An intervening third party could put the kibosh on her plans.

He shakes his head. "Not today."

Roberta nods and saunters to the open trunk. It's filled with fishing gear. "Wow. You must be planning on catching a lot of fish."

"That's the idea."

She smiles politely. "Where will you be staying?"

Ed shrugs. "Not sure. I'll find a place."

Rosey approaches them with the food.

"Oh," Roberta says, stalling for time. "Do you suppose we could split up the doughnuts? Would you have a paper bag inside?"

"I don't want any doughnuts. Please take them back. Thanks for the coffee, though."

Roberta feels her smile freeze up. "Are you sure? We bought them for all of us."

"I'm sorry." And he slams the trunk closed.

"Oh, I almost forgot. Rosey, when you put the doughnuts back, get that package, OK?"

Rosey nods and heads back to the car.

In a conspiratorial tone, Roberta whispers to Ed, "She was so excited about this. She picked them out herself."

"Roberta, please stop giving me gifts."

"But it wasn't me. It was Rosey's idea."

Ed looks toward Roberta's car. "She's a sweet kid."

"The best," Roberta says. "So, how long will you be away?"

Ed is slow to answer. "A couple of days, I suppose."

Roberta feels Ed's skittishness. "That's nice."

Rosey returns with a purple, tissue-wrapped gift. She hands it to Ed. "Hope you like it."

Ed smiles. "I'm sure I will." He splits apart the wrapping. It's a pair of black socks dotted with red cardinals. He holds them up. "And just my size."

Everyone laughs.

"Well, ladies, I got to go." He turns to leave, stalls then half pivots around. "Um...thanks for everything."

Roberta has a sudden, brilliant brainstorm. "I got an idea," she blurts out. "Why don't we tag along? Keep you company."

Ed's brow collapses. "What? You mean to go with me?"

"Yeah. It would be so much fun. Rosey loves to fish." She looks at her granddaughter. "Don't you, honey?"

Roberta doesn't wait for a response. The key is to keep talking and see how far she'll get. "Used to go with her dad," she tells Ed. "I take her once in a while, but it's not the same."

Ed shakes his head. "Sorry. But that's not—"

"We'll ride together. Trade off the driving if you like. Split the cost of gas. And of course, we'll stay in separate rooms. Rosey and I go on car trips all the time. Moment's notice. We're vagabonds."

Ed's laughing now. "You got to be joking."

"Joking? Not at all. Why don't you want us to go with you?"

"Roberta, I don't know you."

"That's a silly reason. Listen, I'll return home, get a few things, and be back in twenty minutes."

Ed glances over to her car. He seems to be thinking, then says, "Sure. Why not?"

"Fantastic!" Roberta says. "Rosey, keep Mr. Mees company." And she immediately turns on her heels.

Ed's mouth hangs open in disbelief. "But wait. I—"

Roberta yells over his voice. "I'll be back in a flash."

Seconds later, she rolls out of the driveway and heads down the street.

Mr. Mees looks at Rosey. He gives her a weak smile. "What just happened?"

Rosey laughs. "You can leave now."

"Excuse me?"

"If it's OK, I'll wait on the porch until she comes back."

Ed takes a deep breath. "You sure you'll be all right?"

Rosey nods.

"How about I get you something before I lock up? Want some soda? Chips?"

Rosey shakes her head. "I'll wait for the doughnuts."

The two walk up the porch steps.

"When you fished with your dad, what did you catch?"

"My favorite was trout. I'd skip school, and we'd go to the creek and use fish eggs."

"Fish eggs?"

"In sacs. I made them myself."

"How did you do that?"

"I'd cut the eggs from the skein, net them, then tie the corners with thread."

"Impressive. Where's your dad now?"

Rosey shrugs. "I don't know. West Coast, I think."

"So you really fish with your grandmother?"

"Kinda. But it's sorta lame. She gets bored standing around."

"And what do you like about fishing?"

Rosey beams. "The surprise."

Ed laughs. "Me too."

Rosey sits on the edge of the Adirondack chair. "Can I ask you something?"

"Of course."

"Are you afraid of dying?"

For a moment, Ed recoils, then rallies. "Maybe a little bit."

"You shouldn't be. The worst is over," Rosey says.

"What do you mean?"

"Being born is harder. And living a lot harder than that."

Ed smiles. "How so?"

"Everything that lives is alone. But when something dies, it's not alone anymore."

"Living sounds sad. Pointless."

Rosey laughs. "Oh no. Life is an adventure. It's like fishing. Full of surprises."

"Where do you get these ideas?"

The girl shrugs. "I don't know. It's just the way I think." She settles back into the chair. "You better leave, or you'll have company."

Ed looks to the street. When the words come out, he hardly recognizes his voice. "Maybe I'll have a doughnut or two after all."

CHAPTER 9

*D*ear Reader, the heart's electromagnetic field extends four feet beyond the body, indicating that when three people are in a car, the electrical charges from each person's heart are mixing with, folding into, or rasping against the others'. What this means can only be conjecture. Still, where there is magnetism, there are poles. Where there is electricity, there's heat. And where there are people in close quarters, there is, I propose, some effect, however subtle, that brings distinct bodies into some kind of synergistic mass, such as synchronized breathing, sine-like heart waves, or weird jumbled brain activity, which may cause dizziness, unexplained outbursts, or quick trips to the bathroom. I could be wrong.

Anyway, our three travelers are now in a car, heading east across New York State. Along with their electrical fields, they are also lugging their respective thoughts, personalities, and a few changes of clothes. It is common knowledge among the principals that as Ed's plan evolves, they will be staying at Saranac Lake, where pristine waters reflect psychedelic risings and settings of the sun amid the mountainous majesty of rolling forests. The place is also only known to Mr. Mees, a short ten-minute drive from where Drew lives.

After the initial excitement and consumption of too much sugar and too little protein, Roberta and Rosey are dully sitting in Ed's car—Roberta in front, Rosey in back.

When Ed glances at Roberta, she seems in quiet reverie with heavy eyelids. In the rearview mirror, Rosey's eyes are closed. Her head is resting against the car door. With everyone quiet, Mr. Mees takes a deep breath.

Dear Reader, a car is not just a conglomeration of parts (metals, polymers, gases, fluids, mini-explosions). It is a hard-shelled extension of every driver in a world of passing scenery, surround sound, and dreamlike thoughts. Sure there is the occasional interruption: a beeping horn, a quick stop, or someone too close, too slow, or too fast for comfort. However, add a couple of passengers, and the dynamic changes. One must become a host ("Sorry about the mess."), ask for permission ("Music too loud?"), be polite ("Anyone need to stop?").

Still, Mr. Mees accepts this intrusion and is remarkably calm. In fact, before his passengers became catatonic, he was oddly enjoying their company.

At first, he suspected his reaction was more of an adaptation than anything else. He could always pull back and remove himself from anything distasteful, challenging, or aggressive. Simply retreat, disengage, and allow others to spew arguments, accusations, or the run-of-the-mill crazy talk of illogical, emotionally charged thinking. It served him well on the job and in his marriage. Good old Ed, standing back as the winds blow. Good old Ed, uncaring, stoic, distant. But he is different today in this car. He is not in avoidance mode; quite the opposite, he is looking forward to this trip. Things may not go well, but he is doing something, trying, attempting, acting on rather than reacting to, which was far more than he ever has. He breathes easily. And for a fleeting moment, a crazy moment, he has forgotten he's dying. He steps on the gas and enjoys the rush of acceleration.

Dear Reader, may I suggest that the synchronicity of hearts in this space bubble has taken hold.

THERE ARE sweet moments in life when one's mind and body are frictionless, free-flowing in time and space, as if boundaries have melted and the universe is a sea of tranquility.

Such a moment is occurring with Roberta as the usual, tiresome chatter inside her head floats across the mental screen and exits to parts unknown. Hovering deadlines. Seriously? Meals to be planned and executed. Who cares? Arguments with Jenna over some friend with benefits. Not my problem. And yes, she is traveling with a man she hardly knows. And yes, she could end up stranded in the wilds of the Adirondacks in any number of scenarios: flat tire, wrong turn, car crash, dead driver. But now, in this languid moment, none of this matters.

Dear Reader, it's difficult to say what's going on in this car as our passengers move along several trajectories: physical, emotional, and mental. Another possibility is they are skimming some higher dimension, infinitesimally close, where other inhabitants suck in the air our principals are exhaling to send back in some rarefied form. On the other hand, in the fullness of nothing (no thought, no conversation), there is peace.

Roberta's phone breaks the silence. She reaches into her purse and checks the caller ID. Jenna.

"Aren't you going to answer?" Mr. Mees says.

"I've called her twice. I hate talking while I'm in the car.

I'll get back to her." And she slips the phone into her bag. "So, how much farther is Saranac Lake?"

"A couple more hours. I called ahead to a motel. They've reserved two rooms. There's a restaurant across the street where you can have dinner."

"Won't you be joining us?"

"No, not this evening. We'll team up for breakfast tomorrow, then hit the lake. I've got a few things to take care of."

Roberta's mind begins to connect some dots. It must be important when a dying man has something to do, someplace to go. She sniffs the air. Yes. There's a story here. She tests the waters. "Your son, Drew, lives up this way, doesn't he?"

A pause settles into the car.

She takes a couple of measured breaths then dives in. "Will you be seeing him?"

Ed's non-response signals to Roberta that she's hit pay dirt. She continues the one-way conversation. "Having children is a humbling experience. Not sure when it happens, but somewhere along the line, we seem to trade places with our offspring and become victimized by them. OK. Maybe that's too strong a word. Still, I often wonder who's got the upper hand in the parent-child relationship. You know?"

"He's not talking to me," Ed says flatly.

"Really? That's odd. I find you easy to talk to. Not like a lot of people who are so quick to judge and give advice."

Ed shrugs.

"My daughter, Jenna, and I talk in parallel ways. Like different levels, never quite connecting. I don't argue. I'm reluctantly agreeable."

Ed glances at Roberta.

"We get along on the surface," Roberta says. "But a lot goes unsaid, unchallenged, misconstrued, you know? Sometimes it eats me alive. It's not fun being eaten alive."

Ed laughs. "Doesn't sound pleasant."

"'Piece of My Heart' Remember that song? Anyway, you have to keep plugging away. So what's the plan?"

"Plan?"

"With your son?"

"I'll head over there and knock on the door."

"Cold call. Good idea. Catch him off guard. Besides, what's the worst he could do?"

"Eat me alive?"

Roberta laughs. "Keep him away from the knives. Did your ex-wife give you any advice?"

"Helen? She doesn't know."

"So Drew and she aren't close either?"

"They talk regularly. Helen is the go-between. Has been for years."

"A mediator? Sounds like a luxury. I could use one of those."

"Mediator? I don't know about that. I often feel outnumbered."

"So, what made you decide to visit him?"

Checking the side view mirror, Mr. Mees shrugs.

"Did something happen?"

"No, nothing happened."

Roberta has her doubts. "Would you like us to go with you? We wouldn't mind."

"Won't be necessary."

Rosey speaks up. "Mr. Mees, maybe you should bring your son fishing."

Ed smiles. "Fishing, huh? Why do you think?"

"Sometimes all you gotta do is be together. Talking can get in the way."

Ed laughs. "How did you get so smart?"

"I don't know. Grandma, can I open the window?"

Roberta looks at Mr. Mees. "Do you mind?"

"Of course not." Mr. Mees says.

Roberta turns her head. "Sure. Go ahead, honey."

The window hums down, and fresh air fills the car.

"She likes wind against her face and the noise inside her ears. I used to worry that she'd get ear infections. But she never does."

Ed nods.

Roberta turns back. Rosey's hand is outside the window, cupping the breeze. Her hair is madly spiraling around her head.

Roberta's heart aches in a very good way.

CHAPTER 10

*D*ear Reader, movement across physical and mental planes occurs helter-skelter with turns, backtracks, and tangential offshoots. But germane to movement is its polar opposite, stillness—those troubling spaces between words, that vacuous silence amid notes, the frightening inertia when the fatigued brain can no longer figure out how an obstacle can be jumped over, dug beneath, or gone around.

This is the condition we find Roberta in at 6 PM on Sunday in a distant motel room where she has stalled, unsure of her next move. But enough is enough. She looks over to Rosey and takes the first step.

"Sweetheart, I'm going to call your mother. Can I ask you a big favor?"

Rosey looks up from Ed's opened tackle box. "Sure."

"Your mother and I had a conversation the other day. It was about Mr. Mees. She didn't want you visiting him."

"How come?"

"I guess she's worried you might become too attached. It didn't make sense. Anyway, I told her I wouldn't take you to see Mr. Mees and that you could stay with her when I had to see him. But this morning, she wasn't at the house, so I brought you along. Then when I picked up the suitcases for the trip, I phoned her, but she didn't answer. I'm calling her now and thinking it may be a good idea not to bring up Mr. Mees. There's no need to lie. I would never ask you to do that. Just say you're with me on an assignment. Which, of course, you are. And that we'll be doing some fishing. Which is true. And I'll handle the rest."

"OK."

Roberta sighs with relief. Next step. She punches in Jenna's number.

"Mother, where have you been? I called hours ago."

"We were on the road. Did you get my message?"

"Yes. What assignment are you talking about?"

"It's research."

"What kind of research?"

"Adding to my travelogues. We're in the Adirondacks. Fishing. Women and fishing."

"You hate fishing."

"Yes. But Rosey loves it. I figured I might like it more if I actually caught something."

"Why didn't you tell me about this yesterday?"

"It was on a lark."

"So, where are you?"

"Saranac Lake."

"When are you coming back?"

"Tuesday. Do you want to talk to Rosey?"

"Yes."

Roberta's stomach feels uneasy. But it usually does when talking with Jenna. She walks over to the bed and gives Rosey the phone.

"Hello, Mom. We're staying in a motel with a pool. I ordered pizza at this restaurant. It was made with English muffins. Gross...This weekend? Sure...OK. Bye." Rosey hands the phone back.

Roberta continues the phone conversation. "Yeah, the food was strange. I had spaghetti, but I think they used salsa instead of tomatoes. A tad spicy. Maybe we'll go to a different place tomorrow. So what are you up to?" Roberta waits for a response. "Jenna? Hello?" And Roberta realizes her daughter has hung up.

So the beat goes on where parents' shortcomings are passed on and reflected in their children, who then become parents to repeat the process, ad nauseum, in endless trials of confusion, disdain, and holiday drama. But there's a bright side. Resilience, an unheralded survival mechanism, is fostered in all concerned, which leads us to Mr. Mees.

In a room four doors down, Ed is peering into the double barrel of his life's pride, joy, and love—the Bernadelli Gamecock, aka Lola. There's no rust, just some minor pitting from the previous owner. That would never have happened with Ed. He's taken great care of the shotgun bought forty years earlier from a brakeman who drank too much and was always in need of cash, especially around the holidays.

Ed lifts Lola to the light. Her bores are spanking clean and oiled. He closes the double barrel and runs a hand over her velvety walnut stock. Lifting the 20 gauge to his shoulder, he peers down the sight, and crooks a finger around one trigger, then the other. Kaboom is heard inside his head. He sighs and puts Lola into the case. It would be nice to test her later. He brought birdshot. But this time, for the first time, she would be Drew's gun.

He glances toward the Winchester. Forlorn next to Lola, it had seen troubled times from his son—left in the rain, rarely cleaned, and too many times forgotten in car trunks and damp basements.

Ed wasn't sure if Drew would want the Winchester. Too many years had passed with never an inquiry, an anecdote, a trek into the woods to shoot beer cans or melons. Still, the 94 model, pre-64, was widely sought after and worth some money.

Ed picked up the rifle. Its compact style was perfectly balanced, and, except for scrapes, the blue-gray steel held a nice patina. He jockeyed the lever. The action was smooth. Yeah, it had been worth cleaning and keeping.

Anyway, it was time to pass both guns on. There were no guarantees where they'd end up when he was six feet under. Too many years of Helen haranguing him about the evils of gun ownership. Too many stories about wills not being followed.

Lastly, sitting by itself on the nightstand, was the Glock and Ed's mixed feelings. Should he take it to Drew's or return it to the glove compartment?

Dear Reader, consider those times when you're cleaning out a drawer, a closet, an attic dresser and find a tossed-aside artifact, an item once useful, perhaps irreplaceable, that remains saved, not for its utility, but for its promise—when you weigh less, when the lights go out, when at some unlikely time you'll have to draw a perfect circle. Such is the case with Ed's Glock—when he may have to shoot it. One last time.

For Ed, it's comforting and empowering to believe some options do not require strength, resolve, or logic. He walks over to the pistol, picks it up, and returns it to the pouch in his overnight bag.

Fifteen minutes later, Ed, with the gun case, is climbing the steps to Drew's front door. His body feels heavy, lumbering. He tries to catch a breath and, for a moment, considers returning the following day when he'd be rested and not zoned out after the long drive. How did every movement become a chore?

At the top of the stairs, he props himself against the door jamb feeling as if the floor is slanted or that he's somehow gotten smaller, shorter. Then, immobilized to the spot, he manages to knock.

His son's voice calls out. "Come on in."

Ed sucks in some air, opens the door, and enters.

"I'm in the kitchen."

The disembodied voice is coming from the rear of the home. Ed passes through the living room, expecting to see some relics—lamp, coffee table, bookcase—from the old house. But nothing is familiar.

Drew's back is toward him. He's cooking something on the stove. "Hello there," Ed says lamely.

Drew turns. His eyes narrow. "What are you doing here? Is something wrong?"

In the four years since Ed's seen Drew, his son's hair has grown long, and he's sporting a beard. "Wrong? Nothing's wrong."

He looks behind Ed. "Where's Mom?"

"She's in Buffalo." Was disappointment showing in Ed's voice?

"Is she OK?"

"Yes." And from a surfacing subconscious level, Ed thinks he may have made a mistake.

"Do you want to sit down?"

"Are you busy?" Ed says.

"Does it look like I'm busy?"

"You're stirring a pot."

"What's that supposed to mean?"

And the familiar sea of misunderstanding floats in. There

would be no blissful homecoming because, after so many years, no one has left home.

"I have some stuff I want to give you. If you don't want it, sell it, throw it in the garbage. Whatever you like." Ed places the gun case on the kitchen table.

Expressionless, Drew folds his arms. Seconds hang in the air.

Ed must have said something wrong. He pivots to leave, then changes his mind. He's come this far. "I'm sorry," he says for no particular reason. "Please. Come take a look."

Drew shakes his head and walks to the table.

Ed unlocks the latches and opens the case, revealing the two guns.

Drew smiles. "Wow."

Ed hopes a corner has been turned. "I want to make sure you get these. Your mother...well, she disapproves of guns."

Drew reaches in and picks up the Winchester. "Where'd you find this?"

"I've had it in the cabinet."

"Really? I thought I gave it away."

"Guess not."

He brings the rifle to eye level and looks down the sight.

"I got some 30-30s in the car. Want to shoot it?"

"I don't remember it being so small."

"Compact."

"Yeah."

Ed stands back. "It's a collectible."

"Looks good. Better than I remember it."

"It cleaned up nice," Ed says.

Drew nods. "A buddy of mine is a gun freak. I'll have to show him this."

Ed smiles. "Sure thing."

He's waiting for Drew to notice Lola.

"Who designed these rifles?"

"Browning." Ed reaches for the Bernadelli. "Remember this?"

"Yeah, that's your gun."

"Was my gun. I want you to have it."

"Thanks," Drew says, not bothering to take a closer look.

"Do you hunt much?"

"Nah. Don't have the time. Work a lot of hours."

"I see. It's OK if you sell them. Your call," says Ed. "Can I take you to dinner?" His voice sounds weak.

"Tonight? Sorry. I got plans."

"How about tomorrow?"

Drew shrugs. "I guess. How long are you in town?"

"I plan on leaving Tuesday morning and going fishing tomorrow. I want to give you the gear once I'm done. Would that be OK?"

"Sure thing. So, where are you staying?"

"At the Blue Skies Motel."

"How about I pick you up around six tomorrow? We'll go over to Harley's."

"I'd like that."

Drew nods and puts the Winchester down. "Sorry about tonight."

"No problem." Ed offers his hand. "We'll talk more tomorrow."

Drew's grasp is firm. In response, Ed holds tight, feeling the warm, certain connection...until Drew's grip goes limp, and Ed lets go.

CHAPTER 11

*a*t 10 AM, Roberta has stopped fishing. Her abandoned pole sits in the well of the boat. Ed's been showing Rosey how to make knots, what size hooks to use, and some suggestions on what lures would work with different fish.

Roberta, meanwhile, has her own fish to catch. Interrupting the lapping sounds against the boat, she dives in. "Have you thought more about being my muse?"

"Muse?" Ed says. "Or victim?"

Roberta laughs. "Victim? I'd never do that."

He calls over to Rosey. "If you feel a bite, tug a little."

Roberta continues. "We don't have to use your real name."

"If you make up my name, you may as well make up the story." He stops looking where the line angles into the water. "Let me ask you something. Why are you doing this? What's the point? I would never want to read about me or anyone else who's... sick."

"Yes, I understand, but you aren't my reader."

"Then who is?"

"Anyone who thinks about it, worries about it, wants to understand how it is handled, if only by one person."

Ed gives a half smile. "Who are you talking about here?"

"What do you mean?"

"Are you my reader?"

"Well, yes. I suppose I am."

"So forget the article. What do you want to know?"

"Ed, it's not just about me. Other people would be interested. And... it might be interesting for you too."

"How so?"

"You get to tell your story."

"I have no story."

"We all have stories. For instance, there's a great story right here, right now, on this beautiful lake."

"So, how does the story go?"

"A man who's, you know, sick, decides to take charge of something rather than be a victim. So he sets out to fish and see his son. And the story begins."

"Aren't you making some assumptions?"

"Yes. But you're not telling me anything. I have to improvise. Off the record. What's going on?"

"Off the record?"

Rosey pipes in. "That means it won't be printed."

Ed smiles. "Good. I don't want to read about myself. Too redundant." He turns to Roberta. "No offense, but you got to stop this. It's pointless. At least, with me. I'm not the guy."

"But you are. I'm sure of it. So why did I crash into you? Or vice versa."

"As I recall, I pulled out, and you swerved into me."

"Yes. But isn't that odd? I've never bumped into anyone before."

Rosey glances over. "Mr. Mees, there are no accidents."

"Exactly," Roberta says.

Ed laughs. "Ladies," he turns his face and points to a thin

red line. "See this mark on my neck. I cut it shaving this morning. It was an accident."

"All right then. You win," Roberta says. "Can I tell you how I see the project?"

Ed reels in his line and casts off again.

"Remember the book *Tuesdays with Morrie?* "

Ed shrugs.

"It's about a reporter who spends Tuesday afternoons with his former professor. The professor, Morrie, has Lou Gehrig's disease, and his body is shutting down. During their afternoons, Morrie talks about his life, telling stories and what he's learned. It's very inspirational."

Ed looks at Roberta. He's smiling. "I've learned nothing."

"Nothing? Is that possible?"

"Yes."

"Now, Ed, everyone learns something. Besides, that's where I come in. I'm the reporter. I ask questions and give the narrative form. Sometimes, it takes a stranger to process what others can't."

"Rosey, how are you doing over there?" Ed says.

"I think I had a bite."

"Sure, you don't want a bobber?"

"No. My dad said real fishermen don't use those."

"Well, on occasion, real fishermen do use bobbers. It's not just about seeing if a fish bites; it keeps the line from hitting the bottom. Fish swim at different levels in the water."

Rosie smiles. "That makes sense."

Ed tips his hat. "Thank you, young lady. I pride myself in the fine art of fishery. Now, if we can only catch something."

As Ed and Rosey continue fishing, Roberta sits back. While ignored, she is not defeated, only challenged. And she likes it.

Dear Reader, how one is coerced varies from person to person. In my interpretations of characters, every protagonist has a particular modus operandi: Ed holds fast, while Roberta, in a maze of crazed maneuverings, stays afoot. Curiously, there is aggression in both positions. Bets can be made here. Who will be the last one standing? Yes, common sense would suggest Ed. He'll wear her down by being obstinate, immovable, or simply distant and unengaged. But Roberta shouldn't be counted out. In a state of perpetual motion, she alights like a buzzing bee, who then pokes, prods, and, as the situation warrants, bites. As I look ahead to the narrative, I suspect each character will be coerced. But then, aren't we all?

With an idea, Roberta speaks up. "Ed, what do you like about fishing?"

"It's relaxing. No time clocks here. Just the rhythm of nature. Floating on the water. Hearing the gulls."

Rosey squints through the sunshine. "Grandma thinks fishing is more boring than relaxing."

Roberta shrugs. "I'm not sure there's much difference between the two."

"No difference between being relaxed or being bored?" Ed says. "It's like night and day. Relaxation calms everything down. But being bored fires you all up. Makes you do stupid things."

"What kinds of stupid things?"

"Getting drunk and watching TV. Nothing more stupid than that. Sitting around waiting for some accident to happen."

"Grandma, Mr. Mees is right. Close your eyes and feel the sun on your face. Listen to all the sounds. Then, you won't be bored anymore."

"OK. I'll try." And Roberta feigns a relaxed state.

With her eyes closed, her mind machinates. Sentences are forming. She's hit the mother lode.

～

AFTER THREE HOURS of fishing and a quick lunch at a hot dog stand, Ed returned to his motel room and nodded off. At 4 PM, he is awoken by a knock on the door. Temporarily disoriented, he looks around the room. Nothing is familiar. The pounding continues.

"Mr. Mees. Open up." It's a man's voice.

"Who is it?" Ed manages.

"The police."

"Who?"

"Open up, sir."

Ed casts his feet onto the floor and walks toward the door. Through the peephole, he sees a man in a uniform. He turns the knob. There are two officers, both young. "What can I do for you?"

"How you doing today?"

"Fine. Yourselves?"

"Is that your Buick?"

Had he forgotten to get the car inspected? Registered? "You mean the blue one? Parked right in front? Yeah, that's mine. So what's the problem?"

"You'll have to come down to the station."

"Station? Why?"

"We don't know, Mr. Mees. We'll bring you back after you're done."

"How do you know my name?"

"We were told your name."

"Yes, but—"

"If you could put on your shoes, we'll be on our way."

Dear Reader, the narrative takes a dystopian turn where the main character is thrust into an unknowable, unexpected predicament. He's been here before, as we all have in the metaphysical pinball game of life where we, as jettisoned balls, bounce against bumpers, funnel through dangerous paths, and drop into gaping holes. The best we can hope for is to handle obstacles with grace and aplomb instead of the mad dash to deny, minimize, or respond with numbing fear or mad flight. Ed is a pro. He remains remarkably calm. Let's face it, he's in the sweet spot with little to lose. Perhaps the only advantage to checking out, buying the farm, and waiting for the fat lady's song.

∼

"Mr. Mees, what brings you to Saranac Lake?"

Ed is sitting across from a corpulent, red-faced officer.

"Fishing. Visiting my son."

"And are you traveling alone?"

"Yes."

The officer leans back in the chair. "Does the name Roberta Hay ring a bell."

"Ms. Hay? Yes, yes. She's a reporter. Does this have to do with her? Is she all right?"

"How do you know Ms. Hay?"

"We met a couple of weeks ago. She wants to... Well, I'm not sure what she wants. She and her granddaughter drove up with me."

"I thought you said you were traveling alone."

"I am. They're tagging along. Hitched a ride. Except for this morning when we went fishing, we're not doing anything together. I mainly came here to visit my son."

"And what's the granddaughter's name?"

"Rosey. She likes to fish. That's why we went fishing."

"Have you ever been alone with Rosey?"

"Excuse me? Alone with her? No. Of course not." And for the first time, Ed feels uneasy. "Where are you going with this?"

The officer looks at some scribbling on a yellow sheet of paper. "How about back in Buffalo? Yesterday morning before you drove here."

Ed thinks. "You mean when we were on the porch waiting for her grandmother to return with their suitcases?"

"You tell me."

"Well, yes. We were sitting and talking."

"And what were you talking about?"

Ed tried to remember. "Fishing, I guess. Small talk. I offered her something to eat or drink. But she didn't want anything."

The officer scribbles words in the margins. "Anything else?" he asks.

"No. That's it." Ed takes a breath. "So when do I get a ride back to the motel?"

"Not just yet. There's someone here to see you." The officer stands. "I'll leave you two alone." And lumbers from the room.

When the door reopens, it's Drew. "Hey, Dad."

"What's going on? Why are you here?"

"I got a call from Mom last night. She went to the house and found someone's car in the driveway. The car was unlocked, and she checked inside the glove compartment to see who it belonged to. Roberta Hay. She then went to Roberta's house and spoke with her daughter, Jenna. Jenna has sole custody of the granddaughter and didn't give permission for the girl to travel."

Drew sat down. "I told Mom that you were in town and that you had stopped by...Dad, we got a problem. You may need a lawyer."

"Lawyer?" Ed laughs. "For going fishing?"

"No, Dad, you may be charged with second-degree kidnapping. It's a felony."

"That's crazy. I'm not spending a dime on a lawyer for

nonsense. Hell, I'll just serve the time and sue the asses off everyone."

"And there's something else—" Drew stops and stares at Ed.

"What?"

"Mom's here."

Ed slumps into the chair. Fuck.

DOWN THE HALLWAY, another family drama is gathering speed.

"How dare you leave town with Rosey. I've had it, Mom. When we get back to Buffalo, I'm finding my place, and the only way you'll get to see Rosey is with supervised visitation. I know my rights."

Roberta stares into space. Maybe she needs something to eat. She feels off, shaky.

Jenna continues. "You're crazy. You know that? Chasing after some guy with my daughter. After I specifically told you not to, never to."

Roberta tries to focus and stay on point. "Jenna, we've been over this. You didn't come home Sunday morning. I had things to do. I called you. You didn't answer. I couldn't leave Rosey alone, not knowing when you'd be back."

"Bull. You called all right but didn't leave any message. Not one word about leaving town until you were already here. You've always manipulated me with Rosey. Not anymore."

"Jenna, to clarify, I'm not chasing a guy. I'm chasing a story."

"Oh, please. A reporter. What a joke! You're an ambulance chaser. And a lousy one at that."

Roberta's eyes seem strained. She looks at a bulletin

board. The lettered headings on the tacked-on papers are blurry. She closes one eye, then another. No difference. There's a wavering sense like she's underwater.

"When that guy's wife found out what you were up to, she went ballistic. Just so you know. Better keep your distance."

"His wife's here?"

Abruptly, the door opens. A tall officer enters with Rosey in tow. "Have the two of you worked it out?"

Roberta stays quiet.

Jenna folds her arms.

He continues. "After speaking with all parties, including the girl, we will file a report and give each complainant a copy. Orders of protection can be petitioned once you return to Buffalo. In the meantime, Ms. Hay, we will escort you to the motel to pick up your bags. You will be brought back here, and the three of you will drive home with your daughter. Agreed?"

No one answers.

Rosey pipes up. "Aren't we going to say goodbye to Mr. Mees?"

Roberta waits for Jenna to respond. Then, in the hanging silence, Roberta says, "No, sweetie." She then looks at the officer. "I need to use the bathroom."

He nods. "Down the hall to the left."

CHAPTER 12

as Helen enters, the room gets infinitesimally smaller, claustrophobic.

Drew leads her to his vacated chair. "Have a seat. Anyone want a cup of coffee?"

Ed watches Helen's face. It's pale, pinched. This isn't going to go well.

Drew waits for a response. Nothing comes. "Alrighty then. I'll get one for myself." And he softly closes the door.

Like animals before impending flight or fight, there is keen observation, assessment, and a weighing of options. With humans, however, matters get complicated as past experience often trumps instinct.

Generally, at home, Ed would stand and walk away. And for a brief moment, it remains an option. But how far would he get? First, he'd have to negotiate an exit from the building, then walk in a vague direction. He further imagines a motley procession following closely behind, with Helen yapping at his heels, leading the charge, "With everything I've done for you."

Of course, there's another way to withdraw from a situation. He could clam up and become an immovable mass whose impermeable density, like the proverbial black hole, absorbs the onslaught of probing questions, erroneous assumptions, and tiresome accusations into a blissful diminishing vortex.

Helen begins. "What the hell is going on?"

Her directness catches him off guard. No warm-up. He feels baited and dives in regardless of his plan of no contest. "Seriously? Do you think I know?"

"Well. Let's take it one step at a time, then. Shall we?"

Sarcasm drips off her. He's always hated it. Too much like old bosses and dead relatives. If it continues, he will walk out. "What do you mean?" he snaps.

"A woman and an underage girl are transported across the state with you in your car. How does that happen?"

"They invited themselves."

"And why did you accept their invitation?"

"It seemed gentlemanly."

"Don't stonewall me. I'm here to help. You may need a lawyer."

"I'm not getting a lawyer. I'll go to jail first."

"That makes no sense."

"So little does."

"What's that supposed to mean?" Helen shakes her head. "Whatever... I just spent five hours with Jenna. She's brought the custody papers. And has phone records and voice messages."

"Any ransom notes?"

"Always a joker. Maybe you should—"

"Listen, Helen. I don't know what's going on with that family. They need to work it out and not get the police involved."

"Jenna was very upset. Worried about that poor child."

Ed looks pointedly at Helen. "The kid's fine. None of this is our business."

"And when Jenna told me about her mother, that Roberta woman, and what she's trying to do to you. Well, she's got to be stopped."

"What's Roberta doing to me?"

"Taking advantage of your situation."

"What situation?"

"Ed, you're dying, and she wants to write articles about it. Who does this kind of thing?"

Ed shrugs. "She has her reasons. Besides, I've told her no."

"And why are you going behind my back?"

"Huh?"

"You know exactly what I mean. You said you were going fishing. Not a word about Drew. After all, I've done for you."

Ed knew it was coming. The subject of Drew. He felt a thickening in his chest. His heart again? "Drop it, Helen."

She sneers. "Like hell. What are you doing? Trying to sabotage my relationship with Drew? It's not going to work. Not after everything you put me through. Drew knows the score. He's not a little boy anymore."

Ed tries to take a deep breath, but it gets caught in his throat. He sits back in the chair. Just relax and have it play out.

"Nothing to say? Typical."

And Ed closes his eyes.

Dear Reader, we go places with our eyes closed. Places impossible to visit in any other way. Unaffected by the gravity of body, mind, or spirit, we are set free. Yet still, with endless possibilities, there's a tendency to spend much time in turmoil where continuous loops of churning rehashes roil. An unpleasant conversation is recalled. Fear is resurrected. Anger is not let go. And, in Ed's case, each constricting thought funnels a chest ache into a chest pain. I want to say, "Think happy thoughts, Ed." But Ed can't. His endocrine system has already released a litany of hormones that are flooding his bloodstream and firing up his organs. His heart is heavy. His mind is racing. And, in the distance, Helen's voice continues.

"I won't let you drive a wedge between us."

Not surprisingly, Helen's obsessive relationship with Drew remains front and center, an unspoken covenant between them. Ed now, as always, shrinks from engagement. It is pointless. Since Drew's birth, Helen has indulged the boy, placated him with whatever he wanted, excused his behavior, and sabotaged any affiliations she deemed an infringement to her, motherhood, and everything apple pie, leaving Ed out of the loop. Meanwhile, the pain in his chest is undeniable. He opens his eyes. "I'm not feeling well," he says.

"I should think so. This is a mess you got yourself into."

Ed looks beyond his ex-wife. They are in a tight cubicle of four miserable, pea-green walls uncomfortably lit by the tinge of stark florescent light. Maybe this is it. The time when everything will cease to exist. No, that's not quite right. When he will cease to exist, just let it be fast and quick.

Dear Reader, there is a discernible moment where life is no more, where the breach breaks, and the pendulum stops. Does it happen in a blink of an eye? Far quicker? Or is it perceived as a slow stretch, where the film, the music, the light elongates into slow motion, guttural sounds, and fog? Perhaps it's like going to sleep or jumping off or soaring high. The pregnant moment we all must live, pass, and die through—the moment of oblivion.

With vague acceptance, Ed wills the pain to worsen. He's as ready as he'll ever be. He shuts his eyes.

In the middle of his dying, he hears a door open. Ed sits straighter and blinks in disbelief. It's Roberta.

"Hey there." Roberta laughs. "I guess this isn't the bathroom. Sorry." With an extended hand, she reaches for Helen. "You must be Mrs. Mees. I'm Roberta. Jenna's mom."

Helen doesn't move. "Yes. I know. Please leave."

Ed looks at his ex-wife. "There's no need to be rude."

"There's every reason to be rude. This woman is ruining your life."

Roberta's smile is frozen. She turns her eyes away from Helen and considers Ed. "Are you feeling all right? You look pale."

Helen nips. "Of course, he's not feeling well. He's in a police station being charged with kidnapping."

"That's silly. There are no charges. I was just told I'll be leaving with Rosey and Jenna as soon as I collect—"

"Get the hell out of here." Helen's voice is shrill. "Now!"

Roberta smirks. "I'll leave when I'm ready. Thank you."

"Ladies. Let's calm down. There's no need to get upset."

Roberta turns to Ed. "I'm sorry about this commotion. Yes. I am to blame. I take full responsibility."

Helen interjects. "Hah. An apology. But how much damage has been done?"

"There's no damage, Helen," Ed says. "Relax."

Helen jumps from the chair. "I'm getting an officer." She jostles past Roberta and slams the door.

Roberta smiles. "Feisty, isn't she?"

Ed shrugs.

"Breathe from your heart," Roberta says.

"Excuse me?"

"That's what Rosey tells me to do whenever I'm upset. Imagine taking breaths from your heart, not your nose or mouth. Like through your chest."

"What's that supposed to do?"

"Gets you in touch with your inner self."

"Doesn't make sense."

"It works, though. Try it. By the way, Rosey wants to say

goodbye, but Jenna won't let her. She says she's going to move and take Rosey with her."

"Can she do that?"

Roberta looks lost. "Jenna is her mother. She has full custody."

"Get a lawyer. Fight for your granddaughter."

"Yes, I should, but—"

"No buts about it. Don't let anything come between you and that kid."

Roberta gives Ed a weak smile. "I suppose."

"Trust me."

A racket is coming down the hall. Helen's voice is leading the charge. "In here, officer..."

Roberta fidgets through her purse and pulls out a folded sheet of paper. "I was working on this at the motel. Please read it." She stuffs it into Ed's hands. "Be in touch. Either way," and she opens the door.

"There she is! Arrest her!"

As the melee of voices sounds off, Ed unfolds the paper.

Blog: The Dying of Ed Mees

(draft)

Mr. Mees is dying. He's received the bad news, scribbled his signature on endless forms, been poked, prodded, zapped, poisoned, and gotten paler, weaker, sicker, to then POW...get more bad news. But he is not down or out. Not even close. We find him today fishing and relaxing on Saranac Lake. He's permanently turned off the television, stopped drinking, and set himself on a course to never be bored again. Will he succeed? Hell yeah, because Mr. Mees is charting new territory, navigating the world from a different perspective. And still kicking.

Before being diagnosed, Mr. Mees was living on automatic pilot with too much routine and too little choice until one day, he packed his car, took a hard right, and headed north. "When your days are numbered, it's time to use different measurements. Forget the calendar, the shrinking days, hours, the regrettable past, the unknowable future, and get to living in the moment." Who am I to argue?

I'm Roberta Hay traveling with Ed Mees across New York State. We met after our cars collided in a McDonald's parking lot, an auspicious accident where a reporter looking for a story met a man with a story to tell. Join us on our journey.

Folded in half is Roberta's card with another handwritten note. Call me. Ed smiles. The woman is certifiable. He then closes his eyes and breathes from his heart.

Remarkably, the pain in his chest begins to dissipate.

CHAPTER 13

*D*ear Reader, why do return trips seem shorter? It's been theorized the road once traversed has familiar markers that, when retraveled, speed up the perception of time. However, the shrinking passage of time doesn't rest with the return trip but with the initial trip, which, in contrast, is felt longer than the actual time. It's about anticipation. In other words, where there is anticipation, there is an elongation of time. Trippy, thought-provoking, and of little use to Roberta as she heads back to Buffalo, feeling the drag of each minute with her laconic, angry daughter in the driver's seat.

After two hours on the road, Rosey's asleep in the backseat, and Roberta remains a passenger. It's odd to sit and be still, but she's getting used to it.

"Want me to drive?" she asks Jenna.

"No, Mother."

Preferring to ignore her daughter's tone, Roberta concentrates on the passing scenery, the rolling fields broken by patches of thick, dense trees.

"What you did to that poor woman is criminal," Jenna

finally says.

Roberta decides to bite. "Woman?"

"Helen." Jenna glances into the rearview mirror, then whispers, "Running off with her husband."

Roberta keeps quiet. Let the nonsense burn off.

"Nothing to say," Jenna snorts. "Figures."

Roberta takes a deep breath. There is so much to say, but what would be the point? "Pretty ride."

"Sure, complain about my Saturday nights," Jenna blurts out, "when you're making a fool of yourself. Mrs. Mees was so worried. She's a saint."

"I think they're divorced," Roberta mentions.

"They are very close, Mother. You shouldn't be involved."

Roberta is starting to overheat, getting a hot flash. "Mind if I open a window?"

"The air conditioning's on."

"I need some fresh air."

"Whatever."

The breeze swirls inside the car. Roberta closes her eyes. It's heavenly.

"She's gone out of her way for that man. Then he goes behind her back to see her son."

"Drew? He's their son."

"He hasn't bothered with the son for years."

Roberta's patience is on the wane.

"I get it now. You and Mr. Mees are peas in a pod. Selfish and controlling. Meanwhile, the rest of us are left to deal with the fallout. Not anymore."

Roberta's shoulders are tensing.

"I wasn't kidding back there. About Rosey and me. Enough is enough."

Roberta's seat belt is becoming more restrictive. The pressure of the strap across her body feels oppressively tight. The tenseness from her shoulders is rising into her neck. She twists her head and hears a cracking noise. "Let's not talk about this now," she says.

Jenna guns the engine and speeds forward. "Ha. Always your way. Just so you know, I've made some calls and have found a place for us to stay."

For a moment, Roberta is confused. A place to stay? But they have a home. Then the realization hits. The "us" doesn't include her. Her heart suddenly is in overdrive. With everything to lose—and remembering Ed's advice—she stiffens and readies herself.

Dear Reader, flashpoints are critical to the story as to life. They are the sparks that cause combustion that triggers an explosion of incendiary words and flying objects. But there's good news. Unsettling the status quo brings change, adjustment, and a new order. We watch with perverse interest.

Roberta dives in. "You are certainly free to live wherever you like. We'll be fine."

Jenna laughs. "You'll be fine. All by your lonesome."

Roberta looks at Jenna. "No, dear. Rosey and I will be fine."

"She's my daughter, Mother."

"Tell it to the judge. The fact is you've been living with me for almost nine years, rent-free, and paying nothing for her support. I have rights, and I will claim them."

"You just kidnapped her. You think a judge is going to listen to you?"

"Jenna, there are no kidnapping charges. And if there were, anyone could see that you trumped them up."

"Are you strong-arming me? What a joke. We're leaving no matter what you say."

"Just so you know, I'll take you to court. Your call."

"Is that a threat?"

"It's a reality."

And a dense silence falls.

Roberta is trembling. Her world, the bottom, is falling out. She's sinking into the car seat.

"Is anyone going to ask what I think?" Rosey says.

Jenna doesn't react. Her face is like stone.

Roberta turns to Rosey. "Sure, sweetie."

"If we can't be together, I want to live with Dad."

Roberta, speechless, is hit with a second blow. What has she done?

Not taking her eyes off the road, Jenna blurts out. "Over my dead body."

Worried, Roberta looks at her granddaughter. "Sweetie—" Roberta stops dead. Rosey gives her a discreet nod with the hint of a smile.

And a glimmer of hope breaks through.

BACK IN SARANAC LAKE, the return trip for Mr. Mees has been delayed. He, Helen, and Drew are out to dinner.

"They're not our kind of people," Helen is saying. "Such ghouls."

"Mom, they seemed nice. Perhaps a little eccentric."

"Bizarre. I drove with the daughter for five hours. The apple doesn't fall far from the tree."

"Jenna? She was kinda cute."

Ed is sipping a Manhattan. Neither Helen nor Drew are speaking to him. He's invisible.

"Drew, you got to be kidding. You like her!?"

"She's pretty. That's all I'm saying."

"Just so you know, she has a boyfriend who's married. Anyway, she tells me all her business but fails to mention she's going to charge your father with kidnapping. I would have driven separately if I had known."

Ed looks at a clock behind the bartender. The earliest he

could get home was midnight. His biggest fear is spending the night in the motel room with Helen. Still, he keeps his mouth shut. The ice is thin.

"Well, enough about them. Sweetheart, how have you been doing? You look tired. Have you been working those extra hours again? I...."

Ed has ordered a hamburger. He's taken one bite. In a previous life, he would have been in his glory: a bar, a drink, a baseball game on the overhead. Now it seems wasteful. He interrupts, "I want to go home."

Helen stops talking, then recovers. "Excuse me?"

"I want to go home."

"Yes. I heard you. A little rude, wouldn't you say?"

Drew speaks up. "Are you feeling OK?"

The room is closing in, shrinking. And the sounds—clinking glasses, murmuring voices, the television drone—thicken the air. "I just want to go home."

"Back to the motel, right? We can't possibly travel to Buffalo tonight."

Ed looks at Helen. "Why not?"

She disengages. "Drew, talk to your father. We're having a nice visit considering the circumstances. And he has to rest."

"Dad, Mom's right. What's the hurry? Get a good night's sleep and leave in the morning."

"I have things to do." When the words come out, he realizes their importance.

"Like what?" Helen says.

Ed looks at his ex-wife and remembers the loose thread, the forgotten point. How did he get so far off track?

He narrows his gaze on Helen.

"What's going on?" she says.

"Helen, your hair looks funny."

She rears back. "Excuse me?"

"Did you comb it recently?"

She pats her head. "What's wrong with it?"

"I'm not sure. Did you get a new haircut?"

"No." She looks at Drew. "Honey, does my hair look funny?"

Drew shrugs.

"You'll have to excuse me. I'm going to the bathroom." She looks around, rolls back the chair, and heads off.

With Helen gone, Ed makes a last-ditch effort. "Drew, I want to say...well, I'm...you know...sorry."

Drew glances away, looking in the direction of his mother's departure.

Ed rushes forward. "I wasn't the best father. I know that. And I can't make up for lost time. I want you to know—" Ed chokes up, then lets it out, "I love you, son."

Drew looks down and fiddles with his drink.

"I came here to tell you. It's the one thing I have to do."

Drew keeps looking down. Discreetly, he raises a hand to his face and wipes his eyes.

Ed does the same.

CHAPTER 14

*D*ear Reader, how much of the future is knowable? Most would say very little. There are only probabilities and possibilities. On the other hand, where there is choice and follow-through, the future manifests. One way or another.

Two weeks later, Roberta visits Ed at his request. It's a marvelous moment, first unexpected, then anticipated. Roberta is prepared to show him a social media blitz. She's secured the domain name *DyingofEdMees.com* and linked it to feeds. Queries have gone out for features. Favors have been called in for promotion. She also has a to-do list: interview, photo shoot, and Q&A. And topics to go over: diagnosis, treatments, support network, feelings, reflections. (The latter being the most interesting.) And there's a big surprise for him—Rosey.

She turns to her granddaughter. "Were you able to write anything?"

Rosey nods.

"Would you like to read it to me?"

Rosey shakes her head. "It's special for Mr. Mees."

"He'll be so pleased. It's a wonderful gift to write down your feelings. He'll be able to read it and think of you anytime."

Rosey smiles. "I know."

"Maybe the two of you can go fishing again."

"No. That's over."

"What? I thought you liked fishing."

"It's OK, but I want to do something else."

"Like what?"

"Make kites and fly them."

"What a great idea! That's something I'd love to do. And your mother too."

"I'm going to ask Mr. Mees."

"Goody. I could take pictures. Or do a video." Roberta looks at Rosey. "If that would be OK."

Rosey grins.

"And yes," Roberta says, "I'll ask your mother's permission."

Ten minutes later, they're at Ed's door.

"I don't know why I'm nervous." Roberta puts out her hand. "Look, it's shaking. There's so much to talk about. On the other hand, maybe I'm excited."

"You'll be OK."

The door flies open. "Hello there." His eyes fall on Rosey. "Great to see you, young lady!"

"Hey, Mr. Mees."

Roberta immediately notices a change in Ed. Is he brighter? Taller? Or has he just come from the barber?

"I got doughnuts. Almost ate one. C'mon in."

The kitchen is full of light and coffee's brewing. "Have a seat. Rosey, would you like milk or juice?"

"Milk, please."

"Coming up."

Roberta settles into a chair and looks around the room.

Her glance gets snagged on a window ledge. She points. "Look, Rosey."

Rosey glances over and smiles.

"Oh," Ed says. "I decided to bring it in. I hope you don't mind."

The bungee birdfeeder man is standing upright on his legs. He's cordless. The colors of the birdseed make it look like an art piece, almost Native American.

"I got kinda attached to it."

"Really?"

"Yeah. Whenever I was outside, I'd check to see if the birds or squirrels got at it. Then I got used to seeing it and decided to take it down and bring it in. Weird, huh?"

Rosey shakes her head. "No. Maybe it's your totem. You protected it, and now it will protect you."

Ed smiles. "That's a wonderful thought."

"Thanks," Rosey says. "Do you have a peanut stick?"

"Sure do." And he plates one up.

"How are things going?" Roberta asks.

"Pretty good. My son and I are talking on the phone. He's going to come and visit in a couple of months. We're going to celebrate my birthday."

"Great. And how's Helen?"

"Helen's Helen. I just don't let her get to me like I used to. And how are you doing? Did things work out with your daughter?"

"Yes. There were a few rough spots but not any longer."

"So we all survived getting almost arrested. Capital!"

Roberta laughs. "Yes, we did." She reaches inside her bag and pulls out her notes. "Anyway, Ed, I'm so excited you called. I've been working on some ideas. Would you like to hear them?"

"How about some coffee?"

"Yes, that sounds wonderful. I know this may seem overwhelming at first. But we have to break it down one step at a time."

"Cream and sugar?"

"Yes, please. Some things should be done first. Lay a foundation." She looks at her notes. "Get the website up and write an introduction."

Ed putters with the coffee cups then hauls over some cream and sugar. "I'll let you add your own."

"Thank you. And if you wouldn't mind, I'd like to take some pictures of you. People like pictures. I think the bungee guy would be a great opener. I—"

"Roberta, I'm sorry if I misled you. I wanted to meet, but not about the project."

"Oh?" Roberta's not sure if she's hearing him correctly.

"I want to apologize."

"Apologize? For what?"

"The whole thing in Saranac. And, you know, Helen."

Roberta laughs. "It was more my fault than anyone else's."

"She shouldn't have talked to you like that. I should have spoken up."

"Don't worry about it. I'm used to that kind of thing. I'm a reporter."

"And another thing."

Roberta wants to keep smiling, but she's getting concerned.

"I want to thank you."

"Thank me?"

"And Rosey too."

Rosey grins. Bits of peanuts are stuck between her teeth and braces.

"The whole thing was crazy. But a fun crazy. Just what the doctor ordered. I don't know what will happen, but I feel good. So good, I don't want to think about dying. Or feel sorry for myself. Or have all kinds of regrets play over and over in my head."

"Yes. That seems, um, great. Really great."

"You know Roberta, you got a lot going for you. You should enjoy it for as long as you can. Stop worrying so much."

Roberta's trying to smile, nod, or do anything not to show her disappointment. She looks into the box, pulls out a Bavarian cream, and stuffs it into her mouth. "Mmm," she mumbles.

"Eat! That's the spirit."

Rosey points to her grandmother and starts to laugh. "Grandma, you got chocolate all over your nose."

Roberta reaches for a napkin.

"Doughnuts are meant to be eaten, not breathed," Ed says.

After wiping her face and swallowing a congealed custard wad, Roberta makes a last-ditch effort. "Ed, we could approach this from an entirely different angle. Not the "Dying of Ed Mees" but the "Living of Ed Mees."

Ed smiles. "But aren't we all living? What would be the point?"

"Yeah. I guess it defeats my original purpose." Roberta says.

Ed laughs. "There are plenty of other purposes."

"I suppose."

"Grandma, don't be sad."

"Honey, I'm not sad. Just regrouping."

Ed goes on. "I've been thinking of making birdseed feeders similar to the bungee guy. I've been experimenting with honey and..."

Roberta stops listening. Without a cause, who is she? A useless old woman. Damn. No. Make that a useless old woman who feels sorry for herself. Double damn. Enough. And she reaches for another doughnut.

An hour later, the company's gone, and Ed's left with a pink envelope. It's addressed: For Mr. Mees. He opens it.

I'm no one special. I'm a seed that grows in dirt and springs to the sky. I'm no one special. I'm a leaf that spreads out and flutters to the ground. I'm no one special. I'm a whisper of wind, a tickle of rain, a ray of sun. I'm no one special. I breathe and think and feel. I'm no one special. I'm better than special. I am all that is. —Rosey

Ed closes his eyes and breathes through his heart. There is no pain, only fullness for his life and everything around him.

CHAPTER 15

*I*t's days later. I'm in my office starting a new book. I hear a voice. It's Mr. Mees. "So, how'd I do?"

"Awesome. I knew you were the man."

"I wish I heard that more often."

"Don't we all. Anyway, I'm happy you didn't die. It would have worn me out. I can get overly involved."

"Happy to oblige." He's looking good, spiffed up in a nice clean shirt. "Whatever happened to Roberta?" he asks.

"She started her own business. Writing obituaries."

Mr. Mees laughs. "Sounds perfect."

"Yeah. She's written a book, *Obits for Fun*. You should check it out."

"Seriously? A bonafide book? But she's a character."

"She's real Ed, just like you."

"And what happened to Rosey?"

"Dear Rosey. She was a mysterious gift who slipped onto the page. I've often thought about her, then yesterday, in reflection, I understood."

Mr. Mees leans forward. "What did you understand?"

"She's that special light inside us, never damaged or hurt, that comforts, forgives, and loves. Always and forever."

ABOUT THE AUTHOR

Award-winning writer and artist, Linda A Lavid, lives in Western New York with familiars of the human and animal variety. She is particularly fond of dried flowers, crinkly and pale, that collect dust in empty jars. According to Linda, they tell stories of lives memorialized in brittle repose of our eternal journey.

ALSO BY LINDA A LAVID

HOWIE IN LOVE: A HATTIE MOON MYSTERY

IF FLOWERS WERE CAKE AND OTHER COLLAGES

OBITS FOR FUN: ILLUSTRATED REVIEWS FOR THOSE
DEPARTED (HUMOR)

MURDER IN THE PACHYSANDRA: A HATTIE MOON
MYSTERY

PALOMA: A LAURENT & DOVE MYSTERY

101 WAYS TO MEDITATE: DISCOVER YOUR TRUE SELF

101 MANERAS DE MEDITAR: DESCUBRA SU VERDADERO YO

ON CREATIVE WRITING

SOBRE ESCRITURA CREATIVA

THE SIMPLE MECHANIC OF INFINITE EXECUTION
(NOVELLA)

BLOOD ON THE PAGE (NOVELLA)

RENTED ROOMS (SHORT FICTION)

OF THE DANCE/DE LA DANZA (SHORT FICTION/DUAL
LANGUAGE)

CATS: WINSOME & WISE (ART)

WOMAN & FLIGHT (ART)

MUJER Y VUELO (ART/SPANISH)